50 HOURS

Praise For The Book

Loree Lough's 50 HOURS is a poignant story that reminds us how precious life is, especially if our world has been turned upside down by cancer. But don't be fooled: This novel will leave readers feeling hopeful, no matter how hard the dreaded disease has hit them.

> Jack Watts, award-winning author of 16 books, including *The Moon* series and *Creating Trump Nation*

50 Hours is a moving story about love, loss, friendship, and last chances. It's a reminder that our lives are precious stories, no matter how long or short. This is a must-read for all of us who have been touched by cancer – victims, caregivers, family, and friends. This poignant and touching tale will inspire hope in the midst of even the darkest hours.

> Cerella Sechrist, author of the popular *Findlay Roads* series from Harlequin

All is well with *50 Hours*. REAL well! Franco is a good dude, and well designed. He doesn't do anything out of the ordinary or unusual, and behaves in a completely believable fashion. And I genuinely like him.

I drug this out for 3 days so I could enjoy the story longer. It's a hard topic, but handled very skillfully. I appreciate the opportunity to share Franco and Aubrey's story.

> Travis W. Inman, author of *Shadows* and *When Love Calls*

You'll laugh, you'll cry... *50 Hours* is an unforgettable tale of healing, redemption, and the cost of true love. With a delicate pen, Author Loree Lough writes an honest and poignant view of what cancer patients face with commendable bravery. A must-read for readers of every kind!"

> Rachel Muller, author of bestselling World War II series, *Love & War*, and the newly released *Phillip's War*

50 Hours is the story of Franco and Aubrey, each trying to navigate a journey through different aspects of death: Franco, who'd lost his wife in a car accident; Aubrey, who's quickly losing her battle with cancer. They're fighting alone until circumstances put them together, and changes their lives, permanently. This book will change lives!

> Rev. Robert A. Crutchfield, Founder FaithInspires.Org, and Christian Growth and Healing Expert at SelfGrowth.Com

A brilliant and heart wrenching story about a determined woman, Aubrey Brewer, making her days on earth count after receiving a terminal diagnosis. Loree Lough took a difficult subject and turned it into a compelling read with light humor to soften the inevitable sadness that comes with a depressing disease. The grim truth about how a person with cancer really feels could only be truly understood by someone who has suffered with the same disease. Emotions run deep between the characters, and Loree perfectly draws the reader in to feel those emotions, right alongside the characters.

> Emma Gingerich, author of *Runaway Amish Girl: The Great Escape*

Loree Lough has entertained me with her stories for many years, but I think with this one we've crossed into a new realm. *50 Hours* is more than a story... it's therapy. Emotion and awareness wrapped around two main characters that make you care for them. The novel is a reminder that life is indeed short, but always worth living. And almost always... one life will touch many others. Great job Loree!

Robin Bayne, author of *Reunion At Crane Lake*

Loree Lough's books are always an absolute pleasure to read, and *50 Hours* is one of her best yet! The story is powerful and poignant on many levels. It delivers stunning visual imagery, characters you will care about deeply and an emotional roller coaster that will leave you satisfied. The story serves as an important reminder of what's important in life, the capacity of the human spirit, and not being victims of our circumstances, regardless of how dire they might be. *50 Hours* is a book you won't be able to put down, and its messages of love and compassion will linger with you long after you've turned the last page.

Kate James, award-winning author of *Sanctuary Cove*, *Silver Linings*, and *The Truth About Hope*

I defy anyone to start the beautifully written *50 Hours* and to put it down or to go on with their own lives as they had before reading about the remarkable, emotional and insightful relationship between dying Aubrey and the lost Franco. As a recent widow myself, the strength, humor and respect between the main characters shot close to home, but delivered so much hope and love that even as I march forward to tomorrow, my perspective has altered---all to the positive. In her last days in this life, Aubrey finally lives out the dreams she's been too browbeaten by her mother and ex-husband to accomplish. She can only do this with help from Franco, who risks imprisonment to see her wish come true. Emerson said, "To know even one life has breathed easier because you have lived, this is to have succeeded." Aubrey and Franco succeeded. Believe me when I say, THIS IS THE KIND OF BOOK THAT WINS PULITZER PRIZES.

Catherine Lanigan, author of *Romancing the Stone*, *The Jewel of the Nile*, and over forty-five novels and non-fiction

50 HOURS

A NOVEL BY

LOREE LOUGH

BASED ON THE SCREENPLAY BY KEVIN JAMES O'NEILL

Can an ordinary man make a difference
in the life of a dying woman...
and change himself in the process?

Text Copyright © 2017 Loree Lough

All rights reserved.
Published 2017 by Progressive Rising Phoenix Press, LLC
www.progressiverisingphoenix.com

ISBN: 978-1-946329-34-9

Printed in the U.S.A.
1st Printing

Edited by: Jody Amato

Cover and Interior Photo: BigStockPhoto. ID:165848003
Copyright: Federherz

Book interior design by William Speir
Visit: http://www.williamspeir.com

Book cover design by Kalpart.
Visit www.kalpart.com

Dedication

50 Hours is dedicated to the memory of those who have lost the valiant fight against cancer, and to everyone whose life has been touched by this maddening disease… patients, survivors, and family members.

Acknowledgements

My sincere gratitude to Kevin James O'Neill for selecting me to novelize his poignant screenplay. Thanks, too, to Joan Kowalski and everyone affiliated with the Bob Ross® name for granting me permission to sprinkle a few of Bob's "happy little quotes" throughout the story. (I hope readers will call or write their local TV stations to ensure *The Joy of Painting* continues airing!)

Chapter One

"DO YOU FULLY COMPREHEND WHY YOU FIND YOURSELF standing before me today, Mr. Allessi?"

Franco stared at the toes of his shoes. "Yes, Your Honor, I do."

"And do you also realize that by getting behind the wheel in an inebriated state, you put others—not just yourself—in dire jeopardy?"

Truth be told, he'd put himself in jeopardy long before he got behind the wheel. His whole life these days seemed like a connect-the-dots game, with each dot representing a new risk. Take last night, for example, when instead of ignoring the taunts of "Get a load of this dude's *wingtips!*" by unruly bikers at the Brew and Cue, he'd started a shoving match, and paid for it with a black eye, a chipped tooth, and bruised ribs.

Leroy Carlisle, his court-appointed attorney, elbowed him back to attention.

"Yes, Your Honor," Franco repeated. He glanced up, but only far enough to read JOHN MALLOY, SR., JUDGE, SUPERIOR COURT on the big wooden nameplate. "You have my word, sir, it won't happen again."

Malloy exhaled a long-suffering sigh. "Oh, if only I had a dollar for every time I've heard *that*..." He frowned at Franco's file, open on his bench. "Nevertheless, you scored 0.14 on the breathalyzer. And since this isn't your first offense, I have no choice but to suspend your license..."

Carlisle warned him this might happen. Thirty days, the bespectacled kid had said, two months at most, providing

Franco looked and sounded—how had he put it?—suitably contrite.

"... for six months."

Six months? *Six months!* "With all due respect, Your Honor, I drive a tow truck. Can't do my job without a license."

Sarcasm rang out loud in the older man's voice: "With all due respect, Mr. Allessi, you should have considered that possibility before driving under the influence." Malloy sat back and folded liver-spotted hands over his ponderous belly. "Under other circumstances, I might have granted you permission to drive to and from work." He looked at the man at the prosecutor's table. "But Detective Rowe, here, says you were so out of it when he pulled you over that he considered calling an ambulance." His slow Georgia drawl quickened a bit as he added, "I cannot in good conscience risk that next time; you might run some young mama and her carload of little ones off the road."

"You have my word. There won't be a next time."

Carlisle jabbed Franco again, this time squarely on one of his sore ribs. Franco drove a hand through his hair and weighed his options: take his medicine like a good little drunkard, or deck the bony-elbowed smartass to his left.

"I could sentence you to sixty days, but since you seem suitably contrite, I'll lessen it to time served and fifty hours of community service. Your fresh-faced young lawyer here can help you choose an appropriate facility." He raised a bushy eyebrow and aimed his steely gaze at Carlisle. "The name of which I expect to see on my desk by this time tomorrow. Understood, counselor?"

Carlisle nodded as the judge banged his gavel, and the bailiff stepped up to the bench.

"Next case," Malloy bellowed as Carlisle stuffed his pen and yellow legal pad into a floppy black briefcase. He muttered something about signatures and paperwork, then crisscrossed the bag over his shoulder and headed for the door. Franco followed like a well-trained pup, hoping he could arrange a payment schedule, because his checking account was as bare as Mother Hubbard's cupboard.

The detective fell into step beside them. "Malloy was mighty rough on you, Mr. Allessi," Rowe said. "Guess it's your bad luck that what folks say about him is true."

Franco didn't care what folks said about the judge—hadn't cared about much of anything lately—but the cop told him anyway.

"He don't cotton to New Yorkers or eye-talians, 'specially drunk eye-talians, so you're two for two."

Franco could have said, "I'm from New Hampshire, and I'm not a drunk." But why waste his breath? God willing, he'd never see Malloy, Rowe, or Carlisle again.

"Well, good luck to you," Rowe said on his way to the exit. "You're gonna need it."

The big wooden door hissed shut behind him and Carlisle led the way to an ancient wooden bench against the wall. Unzipping the soft-sided briefcase, he produced forms from the clerk's office. His cell phone buzzed as he handed them to Franco. "Read these over and sign them." He slid a ballpoint from his pocket and gave it to Franco before hitting the "accept call" button. He turned slightly and put his back to Franco.

This couldn't wait until he'd arranged a ride home? Franco wondered. *What was the guy afraid of? That his flat-broke, eye-talian client would embarrass him by hitching a ride out of town before paying court costs?*

Franco grudgingly filled out the documents while Carlisle nodded, listening to some loudmouth on the other end of the phone who accused him of spending way too much time on "that lousy DUI." Franco snorted. Too much time? He'd stood in fast food lines longer than the young lawyer had spent prepping for this case, and that included the hurried, unfocused interview downstairs in the holding cell!

3

Carlisle was still talking when Franco finished the paperwork, so he tossed the pen onto the open briefcase and picked up the mustard-colored envelope labeled ALLESSI, FRANCO A. Eighty-eight cents in loose change clattered onto the bench, followed by his wallet—which contained forty-three bucks and two nearly maxed-out credit cards—his keys, and a battered, bare-bones gray flip phone that hadn't been charged in days.

The lawyer was about to pocket his cell phone when Franco said, "Mind if I borrow that? My battery's dead and I need to arrange a ride home."

"Make it quick," the kid said, frowning. "Can't be late for my next case."

Right. Wouldn't want you wasting precious time on another drunk. Ignoring the lawyer's dismissive tone, Franco dialed his AA sponsor. *Good thing I have a memory for numbers*, he thought, counting the rings. With a little luck, David Gibbons would agree to pick him up at the courthouse and drive him to Clayton's Auto Body Shop. With a little more luck, Clayton could scare up a job that didn't involve getting behind the wheel.

When David answered, Franco summarized the situation, starting with a reminder that yesterday had been the third anniversary of his wife's death, which started with a boozy brawl that landed him in jail and ended with the judge's ruling.

"Jeez, Allessi," Gibbons grumbled, "what were you thinking?"

"I wasn't."

"Obviously."

Franco heard a heavy sigh, then, "Give me fifteen minutes. And *don't* make me come in there looking for you."

"I won't. And thanks," he said, and returned the phone.

Carlisle pocketed it. "Any ideas about where you'll serve your community service?"

Head pounding and stomach churning, he shook his head. "No, not yet."

"Well, you've got my number. Leave me a message if you think of something. Otherwise, I'll hook you up with one of the soup kitchens downtown."

"Uh-huh." The last place he wanted to be; if he kept going the way he had been, that's exactly where he'd end up one day, and not as a volunteer, either.

"You look a little green around the gills. You gonna be okay?"

"Yeah, eventually." He'd gone from owning a landscaping company to driving a tow truck, and had taken one helluva pounding from the brawny bikers at the Brew and Cue. Spent a miserable night in jail. Took a brow-beating from an eye-talian hating judge. The way Franco saw it, he'd pretty much hit rock bottom.

Where was there to go but up?

Chapter Two

AUBREY STOOD AT THE MIRROR AND TUGGED AT THE brim of her Washington Nationals baseball cap.

She liked the memories it conjured of happier, healthier times, when her greatest fear was forgetting to turn off the steam iron. Better still, the hat didn't make her head itch, unlike the bulky knit skullcaps her mother dropped off every week. And on a day like this, the cap's bright red brim would shade her eyes from intense sunlight, beaming from the azure Savannah sky.

Draping a sweater over one arm, she grabbed her art kit, her favorite material possession, and left her temporary—and final—home. One door down, she stopped at Dusty Myer's room. He claimed to want nothing to do with anyone or anything at Savannah Falls, but if that were true, why did he always leave his door open?

As usual, she found him slouched in his wheelchair, staring out at the gardens. Could he see the beauty out there through eyes clouded by confusion, pain, and despair?

And, as usual, she entered uninvited. "'Mornin', kiddo," she said, stowing her things on the window-facing loveseat. "Not in the mood for eggs Benedict this morning, huh?" She helped herself to a triangle of cold toast.

Frowning, he glanced at it, then drew quote marks in the air. "Mrs. Brewer, Hospice Genius."

Aubrey flinched slightly at the use of her married name. It still stung, remembering what Michael had said when he delivered the divorce papers: "I just can't bear to watch you suffer." If Guinness had a Stupid Reasons to Separate category, that had to be in the top ten.

"No need to be so formal," she said, winking. "Aubrey will do nicely. Or, if you prefer, just plain Genius."

He didn't return her smile. No surprise there. Anger, re-sentment, and bitterness had controlled her at first, too, until one of her art students compared her paintings to the later works of Frans Hals, whose subjects' faces reflected a sense of doom and foreboding. She hadn't told anyone at school about the cancer, so the kid had no way of knowing how ac-curately he'd described her contemptuous reaction to her diagnosis. But that very night, she'd gone through her can-vases and, shocked at how many reflected her dismal mood, hid a dozen or more under a tarp in the basement. Just be-cause her oncologist's prognosis had been grim didn't mean the rest of her life had to echo it! One day soon, maybe she'd share that story with Dusty. Whether he chose to learn something from it or continue wallowing in self-pity was en-tirely up to him.

"I can't decide whether to paint birds and butterflies, or flowers today," she said, effectively changing the subject. "Wait, I know… flowers!"

He snorted. "Too bad you're dying of a brain tumor—"

The words hit like a slap, but she smiled anyway. "Ah, I see you signed up for Doc Robinson's 'Tact and Kindness' class, didn't you?"

"—because," Dusty finished, "instead of painting sun-shine and rainbows, you could write a book."

"Me? A book?" She laughed.

"Yeah. One of those stupid self-help books. Like *Die Smil-ing*. Or maybe *How to Drive Your Hospice Neighbor Nuts*."

Aubrey could have countered with an equally cutting remark. Could have told him that self-pity was an ugly, use-less emotion. But she'd seen his family photos—full-color and black-and-white evidence that he hadn't always been an insensitive, angry snot. Robinson, the hospice shrink, had called this behavior the "lashing out" period. She worried that Dusty, who hadn't even graduated high school yet, wasn't mature enough to realize that his attitude would drive loved ones away, and had the power to exacerbate every symptom of the disease that was not-so-slowly killing him.

"What are you staring at?"

Blinking, Aubrey glanced away from his angry face, focusing instead on row after row of greeting cards signed with little hearts, Xs and Os. At potted plants adorned with bright satin bows. At cheery get-well balloons that bobbed and danced in the AC's downdraft. Her own room, by contrast, looked bleak and bare, save the lonely philodendron, delivered by the family of a patient she'd befriended... on the very day he'd died. She had a notion to give Dusty a good talking-to, remind him how blessed he was to be surrounded by so many people—family and friends and compassionate staff—who cared about him. If she did that, though, she'd have to balance the lecture with an ugly fact: only a heartless fool would imply that a kid dying of cancer was blessed *or* lucky.

Reality hit like a punch to the gut: dozens of friends and relatives would grieve when Dusty was gone. But Aubrey? Aubrey had Agnes, who'd insisted on piano lessons, had pushed her into becoming a cheerleader, and had chosen her college and the courses that led to a career as a high school art history teacher. She'd insisted on chemo and radiation, even though test after test delivered the same prognosis: the glioblastoma brain tumor was inoperable... and incurable. And when Agnes finally accepted the inevitable, she decided where Aubrey would spend her final days, too.

Aubrey envied Dusty, because, oh, what she'd give to know that when she was gone, people would *miss* her!

"How 'bout if I turn on your TV before I leave?"

"Why bother. Daytime TV sucks... unless you're a lazy housewife, or a hundred years old." He grunted. "Or a nosy hospice genius."

An idea formed as she admired his framed family photos, displayed behind the greeting cards.

Aubrey turned on the TV, and while he busied himself cursing and reaching for the remote, she swiped the photo that featured Dusty, healthy and tan and grinning as, arms akimbo, he leaned Jack Dawson-style into the sailboat's gleaming bow rail. She hid it under her art case and hurried to the door, knowing exactly what she'd paint today.

"You're seriously going outside?" Frowning, Dusty clicked through the channels, stopping when a weather map filled the screen. "Channel 12 weather guy says it'll hit 102° today. I take it back. You're not a genius, after all."

"Thanks to the after-effects of chemo, I'm always cold, so predictions of hot and humid is great news to me."

He swiveled his wheelchair to face her. "Question for you, *Aubrey*. We're in a hospice center, where people come to die. So what's the point of chemo?"

"That's for me to know and you to find out."

She hadn't had an infusion in months, and couldn't recall the last time she'd swallowed a bitter-tasting pill. But admitting it might give him an excuse to give up on his own treatments. Almost as bad… the possibility that he'd let the information slip when Agnes was in earshot.

"See you later," she said over her shoulder.

"Not if I see you first!"

Chapter Three

DURING HER MONTH AT SAVANNAH FALLS, AUBREY HAD produced half a dozen paintings, sitting right here on the river bluffs.

In one, she'd concentrated on the Savannah River's shimmering ripples. In another, her focus had been the conical blooms of bottle-brush buckeyes and mottled-green trillium that sprouted beneath them. Today, the vista would form a backdrop for a family portrait. It wouldn't be easy reproducing Dusty's youthful exuberance—especially since she intended to paint it onto his ashy, cancer-abused face, but—

"Aubrey Jane Brewer, what *are* you doing out here in this miserable heat?"

The voice startled her so badly, she nearly dropped the photo. "Good grief, Mama, you scared me half to death." Aubrey snickered. "Oh, wait. Cancer already took me way past the halfway point, didn't it?"

Agnes pursed her lips. "Honestly, Bree," she said, fanning herself with her envelope-sized purse, "must you always be so crass?"

Her mother's inability to cope with the prognosis was as exasperating as her insistence on calling Aubrey *Bree*. At first, she'd blamed Agnes's Old South upbringing, but that only worked for a while. The woman craved control the way addicts crave their drug of choice, and there wasn't a blessed thing Aubrey could do about it. So why waste precious time and energy trying?

Agnes helped herself to the photo. "Who are these people?"

It was a good thing she'd already completed the background, because Agnes had the power to snuff Aubrey's muse as surely as water doused a kitchen match.

"That's Dusty Myers," she said, pointing him out. "You know, the boy in the room next to mine. Hard to recognize him, I know, without the scowl, but that's him. Dusty has a lovely family, but he's doing his level best to push them away." She relieved her mother of the picture. "And if he isn't careful, he might just succeed."

Agnes stood, staring and uncharacteristically quiet. *Considering the possibility that she might suffer the same fate as Dusty's family?* Aubrey wondered.

"How old is he?"

"Just turned sixteen."

"He may just be a boy," Agnes sniffed, "but as you and I learned the hard way, males of our species are born selfish, and think only of themselves. If you ask me, his cancer only heightened an already-irksome condition."

Aubrey could point out that her dad hadn't been the least bit self-centered, but she wasn't in the mood to hear a lecture about all the men who *were,* starting with Michael, who'd filed for divorce within weeks of the oncologist's diagnosis. Her ex had stayed in touch by phone and text message… until Agnes shared the doctor's "terminal" prognosis. Aubrey exhaled a disappointed sigh. "The more things change," she muttered, "the more they stay the same."

"What's that, dear?"

She'd never been the religious sort, but lately, Aubrey caught herself absent-mindedly praying that God would send someone into her mother's life, someone who'd see past her aloof façade and find the heart and soul of the lovely young woman she'd been before her second husband walked out on her.

Agnes picked up the photo again. "I don't understand. Why would he want to hurt his family that way?"

"I'm sure he doesn't *want* to hurt them, Mama." Aubrey slid the ten-by-eighteen-inch watercolor into the art kit. She wouldn't get any more work done today. "Everyone handles the 'you're dying of cancer' thing differently. I may not agree with Dusty's attitude, but I respect his right to it."

Agnes's left brow lifted. Message sent and received? Aubrey doubted it, but smiling to herself, she thought, *A gal can dream...*

"So anyway," she explained, "I had this idea to paint my own vision of this family vacation picture. A bald, pale Dusty, sitting in his wheelchair on the deck of that boat. But instead of bathing trunks, he'll wear a hospital robe. And in place of the sour expression—pretty much the only thing his family has seen since he got here—he'll smile, exactly like he is in this photo." She thumped it for emphasis.

Putting words to her plan made her more certain than ever that it had been a good idea, and she was more determined than ever to finish it before...

Aubrey couldn't bring herself to complete the thought.

"That way, when he's gone, they'll have something tangible to remind them what he was like before cancer changed him. And maybe, just maybe, it'll make losing him a little less painful."

Agnes's brow furrowed. "I declare, Bree," she said, crossing both arms over her chest, "sometimes you're too nice for your own good. You'd better hope your thoughtful gesture doesn't deplete your strength. Sitting out here in this heat, for that mean-spirited boy? You're out of your mind."

Aubrey ignored the slur. After wiping her fan brush on a paper towel, she returned it to its slot in the art kit. If her mother knew her at all, she'd know that painting didn't deplete her, it energized her!

"You look more peaked than usual today. Did you take your meds?"

If she had, she wouldn't have had the energy to walk out here, but nothing could make her admit it. Aubrey had tried taking the 'truth and nothing but' route with Agnes before, explaining how the drugs made her sleepy and weak, fuzzyheaded and clumsy and forgetful. Made her hands shake so badly she could barely *hold* a brush, let alone manipulate one so that she could paint weathered boards and knotholes on a barn wall, downy barbs on the shaft of a bird's wing, the pistils and anthers of rose petals. Last time the subject came up, Aubrey's honest answer had put tears in her mother's eyes. "You never liked taking medicine," Agnes had whimpered, "not even cough syrup when you were little." The scolding had left Aubrey feeling immature. Dishonest, too, as she pictured herself flushing the costly drugs down the toilet. But guilt, she'd learned, was easier to live with than the drugs' side effects.

Agnes snapped her fingers. "Bree, are you paying attention? I asked you a question."

Aubrey had turned forty-four on her last birthday. Why did she allow Agnes's actions to force her to choose between telling a lie and enduring an hours-long sermon? She'd graduated at the top of her class at Emory, earned the respect of peers and administrators at the Savannah School of the Arts. Her mother's *lack* of respect was insulting and infuriating. But thanks to the tumor, they'd have limited time together, and once she was gone, Agnes wouldn't have anyone but her bridge club and Daughters of the American Revolution to keep her company.

Aubrey chose her words carefully. "I'm fine, Mama. A little tired, but that's perfectly normal. Considering."

"Well, of course it's normal. And is it any wonder, sitting out here in this god-awful heat. Now, fold up that confounded easel of yours—or I'll do it for you—and let's get back inside where the air is filtered *and* air conditioned."

"Confounded?" Aubrey feigned shock. "What would the garden club ladies say if they heard you using a euphemism for damned?"

Finally, a smile!

"Lucky for me," Agnes said, grabbing the art kit, "they'll never be the wiser, because I raised a daughter who knows when to keep her lips zipped."

It didn't escape Aubrey's notice that her mother's pace matched her own. Agnes had two speeds: fast and stop. Aubrey linked arms with her mother and whispered, "Thanks, Mama."

"No need," Agnes said. "This old kit isn't the least bit heavy." Nodding, Aubrey guided her mother to a stop.

"Just look at that," she said, pointing at the coral bells and impatiens planted on either side of the wide flagstone path. "Would you mind very much if we sat here for a minute? I'd love to make some sketches, you know, in case I want to add them to the painting of Dusty."

"On a sailboat?"

"Why not? Michael's friend Joe has a sailboat, and his wife keeps plants on board."

"You're the artist." They sat side by side on a stone bench. "What are these called, I wonder?" she asked, lifting a puffy blossom.

"The vice president of the Savannah Ladies Garden Club doesn't know?"

Agnes clucked her tongue. "I don't know *everything* garden related, you know."

"It's an oak-leafed hydrangea. I had them in my backyard, remember?"

"Oh. Yes, I do remember. They were quite lovely. But then, your entire yard was lovely." She squeezed Aubrey's hand. "I'm sure the couple who bought the house appreciate the hours you put into it."

"Michael hated them, especially when the petals began to drop in the fall. Said they looked like trash, littering the lawn, but I loved the way they looked, nestled between the blades of grass..."

"Why don't I drive you over there so you can see them? I'm sure the new owners won't mind."

Aubrey had no desire to see someone else's car parked in her driveway, another woman's curtains in the multi-paned windows… more evidence of all that cancer had taken from her.

She shook the image from her mind. "Do you have plans this afternoon, or can you stay for lunch?"

"I'd like nothing better. Unless they're serving that taste-less, rubbery *chicken* again."

"I know, right? The stuff is better suited for a clown act." She pretended to bop Agnes's head with a rubber hen.

Giggling like schoolgirls, they startled a blue jay from its roost in a nearby shrub and, as it took flight, azalea petals rained to the ground.

"That's Bobbitt, my new boyfriend. He sits in the tree outside my room, squawking. Guess he got bored with that and decided to become a stalker and follow me around the grounds."

Agnes clucked her tongue again. "Well, be sure to keep your window closed. Birds are riddled with parasites, you know, some small enough to flit right through the screens."

Aubrey stifled a smirk. "Yes, Mama." Warm, sweet mo-ments like these were rare these days, and she committed this one to memory. Was her mother doing the same?

"You know," Agnes said, looking up at the old mansion, "I've always admired the architecture of this place."

It would be hard not to appreciate the regal beauty of the 1840s estate house and its surrounding acreage. Overcup oaks stood on either side of it, like silent and stately sentries. An arbor of magnolias shaded the winding drive that brought visitors from the road to the grand entrance, and mighty marble pillars supported the curved portico that gleamed in the noonday sun. How it had escaped Yankee cannonballs was anyone's guess, but thanks to the care of a fastidious maintenance crew, every brick and stone had remained intact.

"It's quite a sight to behold, don't you think?"

Aubrey sighed, more deeply this time. "Yes, I imagine it's as good a place as any to die."

Chapter Four

DURING THE DRIVE BETWEEN THE COURTHOUSE AND Mama's Boy Diner, David Gibbons barely spoke. Even now, seated at their table near the windows, he remained quiet. Except for reciting his breakfast order, he hadn't said a word, but Franco knew it was only a matter of time before he let him have it with both barrels, as his grandpa used to say.

Finally, when the waitress was out of earshot, he stared hard at Franco.

"Well?"

A-a-and there it is, he thought, running shaky hands through his hair. "Okay. Look. I know I should have called before all hell broke loose, but... but I was testing myself."

David grabbed the sugar dispenser. "Testing yourself." He sounded more like a disappointed dad than an AA sponsor.

"I thought maybe I could get through it on my own this time."

"Bull." He let the white granules stream into his cup. "You *didn't* think. If you had, you would've given a thought to what happened last year. And the year before that."

Franco knew he'd messed up. Again. And that he had nobody to blame but himself. Head pounding, he rubbed his temples as David's spoon clanked against the sides of the mug. Had he ever met anyone who made more noise stirring coffee? He didn't think so.

David pointed at Franco's swollen lips and the bloody butterfly bandage a nurse at the jail had taped over his left eyebrow. "So, who cleaned your clock?"

"Well, there was this pool cue, see…"

"Real funny. I notice you're favoring your right ankle. I suppose the pool cue did that, too."

"No. That was the work of the biker, attached to the pool cue." Franco chuckled, then gripped his aching ribcage.

"Busted ribs too, huh?"

"Probably."

"Probably? You mean they didn't take you to the ER?"

"They offered. I said no."

"Idiot."

David couldn't call him anything he hadn't already called himself.

"You're gonna have one heckuva scar when you peel that bandage off your forehead. Maybe it'll serve as a reminder, help you *really* think next time you decide to, ah, test yourself."

"You're all heart, David. All heart." He smirked. "Except for your mouth, of course. That's more like another part of your anatomy."

David waved away the insult. "You know how frustrating it is, watching you get *this close* to earning your one-year chip," he said, thumb and forefinger an inch apart, "and then you go and bungle it by pulling another dumb stunt? Every. Single. *Year*?"

Franco didn't have a comeback for that one. He'd screwed up. Royally. At least no one got hurt, other than himself. David knew it, too.

The men sat in stony silence as the waitress delivered their food.

David peeled back the top of a tiny jelly container. "When was the last time you went to a meeting?" he asked, smearing its contents on a wedge of toast.

It had been more than a month, but Franco didn't want to open himself up to another firestorm, so he stuffed his mouth with food and shrugged.

David counted on his fingers: "Pushing your limits. Breaking the rules. Avoiding tough questions." He salted his eggs. "You remind me so much of my kid, it's almost scary." He used his fork as a pointer. "And that shouldn't come across as a compliment, since he's *ten*."

Touché, Franco thought, gulping his OJ. He winced when it stung the cuts inside his mouth.

"Maybe this community service stuff will finally shake some sense into you."

He'd been acting like a fool for so long, it had become a habit. And yet he said, "Maybe."

"How long did the judge give you to choose your community service project?"

"Twenty-four hours."

"Well, it just so happens I have an idea."

Franco stopped chewing. "Yeah?"

"There's a hospice, a half-mile or so from your trailer— which is lucky for you, since you *can't drive*—and I happen to know they're in need of a gardener."

Before Jill's death, his landscape business had kept the wolf from the door. In the three years since, the only garden tool he'd touched had been the shovel Clayton kept out back for scooping up his dog's poop. It might be nice, working hard again. Working so hard that he fell into bed too exhausted to have nightmares about the wreck that took Jill from him.

"You know the old saying, 'If it seems too good to be true'?" Franco lifted one shoulder in an indifferent shrug. "But you've got my attention."

David explained that his sister-in-law had spent her final days at Savannah Falls. "So I know for a fact that it's a great place. I can take you over there, make introductions."

"I dunno, Dave. A hospice center? You know better than anybody that I'm not exactly a people person. Dealing with sick people?" He winced again.

21

"Oh, quit your bellyaching. You'll be outside, mowin' and hoein', and the patients will be inside—"

"—dying." Hungry as he was, Franco shoved his plate aside, because it hurt to chew, and the bacon and buttery eggs burned the cut on his lip. "I dunno," he said again.

"You'll do fine, if you just do your job and keep your big yap shut. For a change."

Franco grinned despite himself. Had it been good luck or bad that put him together with a guy who never sugar-coated anything?

David slid his cell phone across the table. "Call your lawyer, find out how we go about informing the judge that you've decided to get back into the posie-planting business. Cause last thing you need right now is to violate courthouse protocol."

Franco slid Carlisle's card from his pocket, and as he dialed, David said, "When you're through there, I'll call Mrs. Kane, the director, arrange a meeting between you two. She's a good egg, but she doesn't take any guff, so I'd watch my step if I were you. With any luck, she'll put you to work tomorrow."

"I have a job, y'know." At least he hoped he had a job. Clayton might tell him to take a permanent hike once he heard… everything.

It only took a minute to run the hospice idea past the young attorney, and less than that to find out that a phone call from Carlisle would get things straight with Judge Malloy.

He returned David's phone. "The kid said I should get over to Savannah Falls and sign up ASAP. Said the judge's office wouldn't waste any time checking up on me. And that I need to keep track of my hours, so that when the paperwork comes through…"

Phone pressed to his ear, David wasn't listening, because he'd already connected with Savannah Falls. Franco picked up a slice of cold bacon, and took care not to let it graze his sore lips when he bit off a chunk. He slid the plate close again. Hard to tell when he'd have the time—or the money— for another meal, so he did his best to clean his plate, listening as David explained the situation to the takes-no-guff Mrs. Kane.

"She can meet with you this afternoon," he said, dropping the phone into his shirt pocket.

It was all happening too fast. Way too fast for Franco's taste. "But… but I need to figure out how to get the Jeep out of the impound lot. And get over to the garage, see if Clayton can find something for me to do that doesn't involve a driver's license."

"I'll chauffer you around today. But first things first. I'm taking you home so you can clean up your boozy self. You need a shower. A toothbrush. And a change of clothes." He wrinkled his nose. "You look—and smell—like something my cat puked up."

"Cat puke, huh?" Franco smirked, even though it hurt to do it. "People can call you a lot of things, Gibbons, but tactful isn't one of them."

"Tact!" David got to his feet and tossed a twenty onto the table. "Who has time for tact with you falling off the wagon and going ballistic every couple months?"

Ordinarily, a crack like that would have set Franco off. For some reason, it struck him as weird penance, because he knew he had it coming.

He could only hope Clayton would be half as diplomatic, because he needed that job.

Chapter Five

"SORRY, PAL," CLAYTON SAID, "BUT UNTIL YOU GET YOUR license back, that's the best I can do."

Sweeping and mopping, emptying trash, and latrine duty. Could things *get* any worse?

"Take it or leave it."

Franco had no choice but to take it, so he thanked David for his help and promised to repay him for the cost of picking up the Jeep.

"Oh, you can bet you'll pay me back," his sponsor had said as he drove off. "And you'd better not miss that meeting with Mrs. Kane, either. I vouched for you, remember?"

"Like you'd let me forget."

Now Franco stopped walking, stooped, and scooped up a handful of gravel. One by one, he tossed stones into the empty lot beside the road, aiming for empty beer cans and soda bottles littering the lot. One for what the bikers had done to him. One for the report filed by that off-duty detective. Another for having sunk so low, financially, that the county had stuck him with the inexperienced Carlisle. And one for every dirty job Clayton had just assigned. He didn't hit a single target, and in his aching head that made perfect sense, since his whole life had been without aim since Jill died.

Hands pocketed and head down, he made the turn that put him on the long ribbon of blacktop that led to the hospice center. It came to an end at the semi-circular drive that curved alongside an imposing covered porch. Franco made note of the big white sign that read SAVANNAH FALLS HOSPICE. Made note, too, of the plantings. Roses, rhododendrons, and azalea shrubs flanked the brick porch steps. Annuals in hanging baskets and ferns in enormous stone pots stood on either side of the double-doored entry. His spirits lifted slightly. Fifty hours here might not be such a bad way to work off his sentence, after all.

The hydrangea shrubs were in full bloom, and he could almost hear Jill, ranting that they'd planted them too close to the porch; the only way to keep them from overhanging the wrought-iron railing was to lop them off at the stem joints, inviting fungus or insect infestation, or both. Fat bumblebees hovered among the blooms, increasing the odds that the patients or their visitors might get stung. He decided to bring it up at the conclusion of the interview, when Mrs. Kane asked the typical, "Do you have any questions?" question. On second thought, maybe he ought to keep his opinions to himself, at least for today. No sense starting off on the wrong foot by pointing out all the chores her full-time gardener had overlooked... or ignored.

He counted eight patients on the big covered porch, lined up in wheelchairs or seated in white slat-backed rockers near the etched-glass panels on either side of the entry.

"You the new janitor?" an old man asked.

"They told me I'd be gardening." *Fifty hours of gardening,* Franco told himself. "If I get the job, that is."

"He lifted a withered hand and snapped off a weak salute. "Hope to see you around."

Inside, Franco made his way to the reception counter, stated his name, and said he had a two o'clock meeting with Mrs. Kane. While waiting for the young woman to announce him, he walked in the direction of the sunshine that streamed through huge windows on the far side of a well-furnished sitting room.

Not a sitting room, he realized, inspecting the glass ceiling vents, but a sun-room that boasted an entire wall of French doors that led to a flagstone terrace. Fingerprints and pollen created a filmy haze on every pane, but it was a hundred times nicer than the falling-down nursing home where his grandparents had died. His watch beeped, telling him it was meeting time.

He walked back inside. No receptionist, and no one who fit David Gibbons' description of Mrs. Gruff. He wasn't surprised. In a place like this, where people spent their last days, she could be tending to any one of a dozen emergencies.

He spotted a water cooler near the elevators, and emptied a small conical cup in one gulp.

As he crumpled it, the old guy from the porch wheeled up. "Drownin' your sorrows, eh?"

Franco met his rheumy eyes. "Uh…"

"Water ain't my go-to drink when things get bad." He waved Franco closer. "You want somethin' stronger, I'm in room 202." He winked one rheumy blue eye. "They got rules about booze in here, but I say screw 'em. I'm here to die, not to get clean. Besides, this place costs a small fortune. If I wanna go out half-tanked, what business is it of theirs, right?"

A stash, huh? Franco inhaled proof of it on the old guy's breath. He licked his lips. *Nice to know…*

"So did the old bat give a reason for not hiring you?"

"I, ah, Mrs. Kane hasn't interviewed me yet."

He pointed at Franco's watch. "What time is it?"

"Two-o-eight."

"She's ten minutes late for everything. Roll me over there to the divan and sit with me for a minute. I'm gettin' a crick in my neck, lookin' up at you."

His grandmother had called it a divan too. Grinning slightly, he gripped the chair's handles and fulfilled the man's request.

"Guess you're wondering why I made you push me, instead of using my controls."

Franco shrugged. "Conserving battery?"

"By jiminy, you got it!" Cackling, the old fellow slapped a bony knee. "What's your name, son?"

"Franco. Franco Allessi."

"Allessi. Eye-talian, eh?" Extending a wrinkled, arthritic hand, he said, "Name's Earl Bronson. You know, as in Charles, star of all those old get-revenge movies."

The strength of Earl's handshake belied his condition. "So tell me, Franco Allessi, how long since your last drink?" The question caught him off guard.

"I saw your pupils dilate when you heard there was booze in my room."

Franco didn't know what awful disease had put Earl at Savannah Falls, but it sure as heck wasn't brain-related!

"Workin' on a stay-clean chip, are you?"

Sober, he rarely talked about himself; if Earl had asked the question a couple nights ago at the Brew and Cue...

"Allessi. Was I right? Italian?"

"Yep."

"Just your dad, or your mother too?"

"Just dad. Mom is Irish."

Earl chuckled. "Nice mix. Explains your dark eyes and fair skin. Not sure where you got those muscles, though."

"I exercise some." Hefting 18-wheeler tires, assisting the creaking hoist of Clayton's ancient tow truck, even steering the old beast to and from pickups was a workout. The shop served as the perfect example of the old adage, "the cobbler's children have no shoes."

"Mr. Allessi?"

Franco got to his feet as Earl tipped a salute again. "Well, well, well. Good afternoon to you, my dear always-late Mrs. Kane."

"Good afternoon to you too, Earl." She tidied his red-plaid lap blanket. "Your daughter will be here in an hour. I suggest a nap. And some mouthwash." Straightening, she added, "A word to the wise? You might want to warn your supplier that I'm on to him… or her. And that if I find your stash—"

"Can't find what doesn't exist, ma'am," Earl snickered, held a hand alongside his mouth and said to Franco, "That daughter of mine means well, but she's a snob and a prude, and don't approve of my embibin'."

"Lovely breeze on the patio today," Mrs. Kane said. "They're calling for rain, so as soon as you've gargled, you might consider enjoying it."

Earl thumbed his wheelchair's joystick forward. "Nice meetin' ya, Franco, and good luck gettin' the job!"

The director extended an arm, inviting Franco to follow her down the hall. "He's quite the character, isn't he?"

Franco followed her into the office. "Yeah, he's something, all right."

She closed her office door. "Please, have a seat, Mr. Allessi."

"No need to stand on formality. Franco is fine."

Instead of making the same offer, she handed him what appeared to be an employment application and a pen. "I see no need for a background check. David Gibbons assures me you're an upstanding citizen—when you're sober—and that's good enough for me." Nodding at the form, she added, "That's mostly so we can contact you in the event you're late for work… or something."

He got her message, loud and clear: show up on time, or the judge gets a phone call.

"At David's suggestion, I spoke with your employer, and he assures me you're free to work whenever we need you. So if you're amenable, you can start today and work full-time hours, since Amos—our regular janitor—is on vacation."

It was Wednesday. By his calculations, he could shave nearly twenty hours from his sentence, simply by saying yes.

"Oh, I'm amenable. *Way* amenable," he said, bending over the form. "It'll take me half an hour or so to jog home and change clothes. Once I'm back, I can work until dark."

"Or you could borrow a pair of Amos' coveralls."

The image of a grease-stained jumpsuit flashed in his mind. Too much like prison garb for Franco's taste.

"Thanks, but I don't mind going home."

Mrs. Kane sat quietly sifting through patient files while Franco printed his name, address and phone number, educational background, and military service history onto the form. She barely gave it a glance when he handed it to her.

"In the past, our experience with community service candidates has been limited to students, retired people, even the clergy." Hands folded on her desk, she pursed her lips. "You're the first who has come to us as the result of a court order. So even though David speaks highly of you, I feel duty-bound to make a few things clear."

Franco swallowed, wishing he'd refilled that pointy cup before chucking it into the trashcan beside the water cooler.

"A week from Monday, when Amos returns, if he doesn't have things for you to do, you'll likely be assigned to work with Carl in our maintenance department. Mopping. Collecting trash. Windows. Cleaning the public area restrooms…"

He did his best to mask his discontent; except for the windows, she'd pretty much recited Clayton's chore list.

"You're not to enter patient rooms, ever, under any circumstances, unless a salaried Savannah Falls staff member accompanies you. And if, at any time, I have reason to suspect you've been drinking, I'll have no recourse but to have you escorted from the property."

And call the judge, who would throw him in the slammer.

"I know Judge Malloy, a fair but by-the-book gentleman. He golfs with my husband, you see. I trust you won't give me reason to call him."

She seemed as uncomfortable outlining the rules as he was listening to them. But even if she'd delivered them in a venomous tone, he would have taken it on the chin. This was a beautiful, peaceful old place. No matter what they asked him to do, it would beat jail time or serving out his sentence someplace else. Besides, his own actions had put him there. He'd consider it penance for past sins. And God knew he'd committed plenty of those.

Mrs. Kane stood behind her desk. "Any questions?"

He got to his feet and thought of the hydrangeas. "Not a question, really, so much as an observation."

One eyebrow arched on her forehead. "Oh?"

"Those hydrangeas out front are pretty old. When they were planted, I imagine they were a good bit back from the wheelchair ramps. But now, they're overhanging the railing, and I noticed they're attracting bees. Lots of bees. If I trim them back, it'll pretty much eliminate the chances a patient or visitor might get stung. The bees are more interested in honey than people, so they'll stay with the flowers."

"Oh my, yes," she said, one hand pressed to her chest. "I dodge those annoying things every day on my way in and out of the building. By all means, do whatever it takes to get them under control."

"Okay. Just so you know, pruning them that far will leave a huge bare spot, and the shrubs will look pretty raggedy for the rest of the season."

"I understand, and it's a price worth paying, if you ask me."

She walked with him to the lobby, and halfway there, said, "David mentioned that you and your wife owned a landscaping company before…" A sympathetic smile lifted one corner of her mouth. "I'm sorry for your loss." Then, standing beside him on the porch, she glanced at the hydrangeas and swatted at a bee. "Oh yes, by all means, take care of these things."

Franco nodded and made his way down the steps. "I live right up the road," he said, looking up at her. "When I get back, where would you like me to start? I mean, since Amos isn't here to direct me."

A bee buzzed around her head, and she ducked. "I'll give you three guesses! But if there's time when you've finished here, I'd love for you to deadhead those roses." She glanced at the shrubs that lined the walk. "They look so sad and pathetic."

He promised to return within the hour and, hands pocketed, headed for the road. By his estimation, he had a good five hours of daylight left. More than enough time to take care of the hydrangeas and the roses, too. And maybe scout out the place, find out what sort of tools the famous Amos kept on hand.

Halfway down the drive, he passed two nurses' aides helping patients maneuver the path that zigzagged through the trees. A blue jay dive-bombed his head, and as it flew to the treetops, he saw a dead limb hanging precariously from a high crotch in a towering Yellow Buckeye. Industry pros called branches like that widow-makers, with good reason. The hydrangeas and roses would have to wait, he decided.

First chance he got, he'd call David to say thanks, because this might not be such a horrible way to work off his fifty hours, after all.

Chapter Six

FRANCO PALMED THE SHEARS AND REACHED FOR A spent bloom. *Ten hours down, forty to go,* he thought, giving it a snip.

He heard a soft thump above his head and looked up at the blue jay that had landed on the rain gutter. The same jay, he knew, because it had a peculiar part in the middle of its crest.

"Hey. Are you following me?"

The bird squawked and drew Franco's attention to movement in a third-floor window, where a woman, her head wrapped in a flowery scarf, stared into the overcast sky. He'd seen that pensive, faraway expression before. His grandmother had fought hard to deny the impact of the congestive heart failure that had slowly eroded her formerly active lifestyle, but after accepting the cold, hard facts…

The woman must have sensed him staring. She looked down and frowned, and he read her lips. "What are *you* looking at, jerk?"

The jay called out, as if agreeing with her. She stepped out of sight as the curtains dropped back into place, and the bird flew off, this time narrowly missing his head. "Jeez, watch where you're goin', birdbrain," Franco said, scraping his arm on a thorn as he ducked. Tucking the shears into his back pocket, he inspected the bloody gash, just above the cuff of his right glove.

The jay lighted on the railing, head tipping left and right, as if studying the injury.

"*Now* who's the jerk?"

A low, throaty *putt-putt-putt* was its response.

"Sorriest excuse for an apology I've ever heard."

Good thing he'd stuffed a bandanna into his pocket that morning; Franco dropped the gloves at his feet and used it as a temporary bandage.

When he donned the gloves again and got back to work, the bird took flight once more and joined the cacophony of calls so typical of jays. His grandfather used to say, "I can predict rainy weather just by listening to those loudmouthed birdbrains." A fat raindrop hit the bill of Franco's baseball cap as he clipped the last spent bloom. He returned the shears to his pocket, raked up the deadheads, and aimed the wheelbarrow toward the shed.

It was raining hard by the time he raced back to the main building. Carl, the maintenance supervisor, was struggling to maneuver an unwieldy stepladder and his heavy toolbox to the shed. Franco relieved him of the red kit and fell into step beside him.

"How long is *this* supposed to last?" Carl asked, squinting into the downpour.

"No idea. Didn't have a chance to watch the news this morning."

Carl gave him a quick once-over. "What happened to your face?"

"Sat on the wrong stool at the Brew and Cue."

"Dang. Can't remember the last time I went into that place.

Is it still dark as a tomb in there?"

"Except for the beer signs, pretty much."

"Where you from... not Georgia, with that accent!"

"New Hampshire."

"Ducking out of the frozen north before winter sets in, huh?"

"Moved here three years ago." *Three years and two days.*

"Well, if you're done with gardening stuff for the day, I sure could use a hand inside."

"Sure." He'd almost said, *"Whew!"* because he didn't feel like talking about Jill. Or alcoholism. Or DUIs. Or jail time.

"That shiftless bonehead who works for me didn't collect the trash last night," Carl said, "and the garbage truck picks up at dawn. I might just get home on time for a change if you do it for me."

"Glad to," he fibbed. Anything to shave more time from his sentence, and spare him a long walk home in this downpour.

"Use the big green can—if I know Wayne, he left it near the service elevators—to save yourself a dozen trips to the dumpster. There's a doo-hickey on the side that holds replacement bags, a hand broom and dustpan, you know, in case you miss." He started for the door, then turned to add, "Piece of advice: wear your work gloves. Oh, and one more thing: take care not to ding any of Kane's precious woodwork."

"Gotcha. Thanks."

"If you need me, I'll be in the basement. Got a hot date with a leaky washing machine." He groaned, took off his cap, and dragged the back of his hand across his forehead as he disappeared around the corner.

Franco decided to start in the basement and worked his way up to the third floor, ducking into the public restrooms, dumping castoff paper cups that had collected in the stainless cans beside each water fountain. Easy, lightweight work that required little concentration. He hadn't eaten since breakfast, and his stomach had been rumbling for hours. Thankfully, the wobbling wheels drowned it out. He did a quick rundown of things in his fridge and pantry. Even the four-for-a-dollar frozen dinners he'd picked up at Wal-Mart would taste like filet mignon right about now.

One of the nurses approached and asked if he minded emptying the wastebaskets in a couple of the patient rooms. Since she had to accompany him, Franco wondered why she didn't just do the job herself. *Must be some dumb rule about that, too,* he thought.

"The patients in the last two rooms are down in the solarium," she said. "You're okay on your own for a couple minutes?"

In other words, *"You won't rob them blind if I'm not there to keep an eye on you, right?"*

"Sure. No problem."

She'd barely rounded the corner when he heard an angry, gravelly voice coming from one of the rooms.

"You people are all alike. Spoiled, self-centered, superi—"

A woman's voice said, "Get out of my room. Get out, *right now.*"

"No way, lady. I'm not goin' nowhere 'til I get these blinds fixed. How'd you break 'em, anyway?" he growled. "Got no respect for other people's stuff, that's what, I'll bet. Typical."

A moment of silence was followed by, "If you don't leave, right now, I'll call security."

"So call 'em. Who they gonna believe, some whiny rich broad, or some poor slob just tryin' to do his job?"

Franco thought the guy was pretty callous, browbeating a dying patient that way. But he had no intention of getting involved in an altercation between a staffer and a resident, not even a spoiled, self-centered, whiny resident. *Just keep your head down and do your job,* he told himself.

"I'm not going to say it again. *Get. Out.*"

"Find something else to break, lady. Like I said, ain't goin' nowhere 'til the job's done. Might as well get that through your thick, bald—"

Franco heard a loud crash, followed by a shaky, "Oh no! *Now* look what you've done!"

"Your fault, not mine," the man said, "for distracting me with your nagging."

"My artist's kit…"

"Aw, quit your blubbering. You're made of money—or your family is, or you couldn't afford this place—so you can replace that beat-up old wooden box, easy."

She was… was she *crying*?

Franco pushed the container against the wall and stepped into the doorway. Sure enough, the woman was on her hands and knees, hugging a briefcase-sized wooden container to her chest, and weeping softly.

"What's going on in here?" he demanded.

The workman looked him over. "Aw, elbowed that flimsy piece of junk by accident, is all," he said. "Not my fault she left all her fancy crap on it. Her fault, anyways, peckin' at me like an old hen."

Franco took note of shattered figurines, a now-unpotted philodendron, picture frames, and books scattered all around her. "Let me get it," he told her. "There's a lot of broken glass, and you might cut yourself."

He stooped, began plucking shards of glass from the carpet and depositing them into his cupped palm. If this was Wayne, he'd earned Carl's *bonehead* title. And—if this was Wayne— Franco aimed to find a way to let Carl know that not only did the bum shirk his duties, but he bullied the patients when no one was looking, too.

"Yeah, that's right," the guy said, "better *you* get all cut up than this rich bi—"

Franco fixed a no-nonsense glare on the man. "Hey. No need for that language, or that tone, either, okay buddy?"

He met her wide, teary eyes and instantly recognized her as the woman in the window. She was shaking and pale as a ghost, and something told him it had less to do with her condition than what had just happened.

He helped her up, led her to the nearest chair. "You okay? Want me to get a nurse?"

"No. I'm fine," she said, her voice weak and trembly. "I just want you out of my room. *Both* of you. *Now.*"

"You do what you want, dude," the guy bit out, "but I'm not goin' anywhere 'til I've finished—"

Franco grabbed him by his shirt's lapels and plucked him from the ladder. The patch on his pocket said *Keith.* The guy reminded him of the bikers, only bigger, broader, heavier. They'd taken a lot of pleasure using him as a punching bag. He'd more or less earned the beating, thanks to his big mouth and smartass attitude. But this guy? This guy was bullying a fragile, dying woman, and it raised his hackles.

"Oh, you're finished, *dude,*" he said, drilling a thick finger into the name patch, "you're definitely finished."

Keith's right hand formed a fist, and in an instant of heated eye contact, it looked as though he might cock it back and let it fly. Instead, he grimaced, then stomped down the hall. *Marching straight for the main office to report me, no doubt,* Franco thought. Well, it had been nice while it lasted.

He glanced at the woman. She looked so small, so vulnerable sitting there in the big chair, clutching that wooden box to her chest. Would she back him up if Mrs. Kane reamed him out over this?

"Before I leave, at least let me get the glass cleaned up, so you won't cut yourself," he said. Hand up as if taking an oath, he added, "And then I'll get out of your hair."

When he realized his faux pas, Franco slapped the back of his neck. "Sheesh. Sorry, ma'am. I didn't mean anything by that."

She shook her head, and when she did, the scarf slipped from her head, exposing sparse wisps of blond hair. It reminded him of a dandelion puff—after a child had blown some of the seeds from the stem. She quickly tugged it back into place. "Just go," she whispered, struggling to her feet. "Please. I'll be careful around the glass."

But he couldn't just leave her here with all this broken stuff. What if she was taking one of those medications that thinned the blood? Even a small cut in the wrong place could be deadly. And it seemed to him it would be all kinds of wrong for her to die like that. Eyes on his work, he continued plucking the broken glass from the floor.

"Are you stupid *and* stubborn?"

When he looked up, she repeated, "I. Said. Get. *Out.*"

It was the plaintive *"Please?"* that she tacked on, as if by habit, that finally put him on his feet. Both hands in the air this time, Franco backed out of the room and headed straight for Kane's office. Maybe, if he seemed—what had Carlisle and the judge called it—*suitably contrite*—she'd come and stay with the woman while he finished cleaning up her room.

One thing was certain: no matter what the boss said or did, Franco had a feeling he'd see that sad, helpless expression long into the night.

Chapter Seven

AUBREY DECIDED TO TAKE DR. ROBINSON UP ON HIS offer to stop by, any time.

Hopefully, he could help her make sense of the way she'd behaved. Crying and cowering had never been her style, so why had she done both today? The big, insolent workman had made a mess, to be sure, but the broken things could be replaced. Her dignity could not. God willing, Robinson could help her get it back, at least as much as this ghastly cancer would allow. The tumor may well have dictated the manner of her death, but she had no desire to go out cringing and recoiling like a frightened child every time she didn't get her way.

She'd barely closed the office door behind her when the secretary said, "Hi, Aubrey. Sorry, but I don't see your name in the book."

"It isn't. I just hoped he'd have a minute or two to answer a question."

She spotted the cheery multicolored scarf, crocheted by Dusty's grandmother, hanging from the coat rack. That was about the best reason she could think of to find another time to speak with the doctor.

"Should I have the doctor stop by your room on his way out?"

Robinson's wife and twin sons saw too little of him as it was. "No," she said. "I just stopped by to…" *To find out why I behaved like a toddler.* "… to say hi."

"I'll let him know you stopped by."

Aubrey thanked her and left the office. But she didn't want to return to her room, where one look at the mess on the floor would remind her what a mess *she'd* been. She felt especially bad about the way she'd treated the maintenance man. He hadn't caused the problem. Quite the contrary… if he hadn't stepped in when he did, who knew what further damage that brute *Keith* might have caused.

She made her way to the solarium, the one place at Savannah Falls where she might find a sense of balance. Before suppertime, any number of patients and family members might be there, playing cards, reading, chatting quietly in the bright, wide-open space. After that, it remained empty, save the occasional bird that sneaked in while the glass ceiling panels were open. Aubrey wished it was nine or ten o'clock.

Off-key plinks and plunks told her Earl had rolled his wheelchair up to the white baby grand. He knew three songs: "Chopsticks," "Goodnight Irene," and—

"Aubrey!" he said. "Pull up a chair and help me play 'Heart and Soul'!"

"We need a new song," she said, patting the instrument's now-closed lid, "because I'll bet that one has left permanent hammer strikes on these poor old strings."

"Aw, quit your grumbling, Brewer, or those nice folks will get the idea you're dying or somethin'."

She followed his glance to the other side of the solarium, where a middle-aged couple tried to coax a dozing young man into helping them find the missing piece of their jigsaw puzzle.

"You're too much," she said, giving his shoulder a squeeze.

"Honesty is always the best policy." He aimed an arthritis crooked forefinger at the ceiling. "Especially with the Grim Reaper runnin' around here, loppin' off heads."

"Well, aren't you just a ray of sunshine on this rainy evening," she teased.

"Sit down, will ya? I'm getting a crick in my neck, staring up at you."

Aubrey dragged a chair closer to the piano, fingers curved over the C, A, F, G, and D keys.

"You start," she said, "and I'll join in."

An old woman in the corner perked up and started clapping, and the couple rolled the young man's wheelchair closer.

"Oh great," Earl muttered, "here comes See-See."

"Who?"

"Only thing she says. Ever." He leaned closer and imitated her gravelly two-note song. "See-See, See-See." He sighed. "It'd drive me to an early grave," he said with a cackling laugh, "if I didn't already have one foot in it."

Aubrey had seen the woman, but only from a distance. Without exception, she scooted through the halls in a wheelchair constructed entirely of white PVC, no doubt to protect her delicate bones and the facility's elegant furnishings and original woodwork in the event of a collision. Until today, she'd never been close enough for Aubrey to hear the grating, two-note chant.

Earl banged out the first notes of the song and took a deep breath. "Heart and soul," he began, "I fell in love with you…"

He played the song three times, and probably would have repeated it again if Aubrey hadn't said, "I need to get back to my room. Little accident that I need to clean up."

Earl harrumphed. "That's what diapers are for!"

Laughing, Aubrey gave him a sideways hug. "Not that kind of accident, you silly old man!" Rising, she offered her chair to See-See's daughter and bid them all a good evening.

If you had any sense, you'd stop by Mrs. Kane's office. But with her luck, the woman would send the new maintenance guy to clean up the mess in her room, and Aubrey had no idea how she'd face him. It would be easy enough to clean things up herself—if she didn't fear a dizzy-spell-induced face plant. Better to avoid that side of the room until the regular cleaning crew came through in the morning. Until then, she'd wear her solid-soled deck shoes, not flip-flops, and certainly not bare feet.

Aubrey squared her shoulders, determined not to let it get to her when she got another eyeful of the rubble, took a deep breath, and opened the door.

What she saw froze her in place.

Her room was clean and clutter-free—tidier, even, than before the smart-mouthed workman knocked over her étagère. The books, picture frames, and candles had been artfully arranged above a new TV and stereo unit, and beneath them, her art kit, smack in the middle of the bottom shelf. Every splintered picture frame had been replaced, every shard of glass vacuumed up.

If she hurried, Aubrey could catch Mrs. Kane before she left for the day. She wanted to find out which thoughtful staffer had gone the extra mile to create order and calm where chaos had been.

"Oh, thank goodness you're still here," she said, sitting across from the director's desk.

"Aubrey, you're all flushed and out of breath." Mrs. Kane rushed to her side. "Let me call the—"

"No, no, I'm fine. Well, as fine as I'm ever going to be. I stopped by to find out who you assigned to clean up my room, because I'd like to say thank you in person. What a great surprise it was, finding all that wreckage gone! I went for a walk… afterward. To clear my head, sort out why I had made such a fuss about… about *stuff*. Because at this stage of my life, what does it matter, you know?"

"No, I'm afraid I don't know." Mrs. Kane returned to her chair. "What *are* you talking about?"

Aubrey sat, blinking and confused. Why would Mrs. Kane have a problem telling her who'd performed this act of kindness?

"That workman, *Keith*, who came to fix my broken blinds? He is by far *the* most disrespectful contractor I've had the displeasure of meeting. He flew into a rant, and to be perfectly honest, I have no earthly idea why. He knocked over the shelving unit in my room. If not for the new janitor who happened by, I don't know how much more—"

"Wait. Give me a minute to catch up, here." Mrs. Kane leaned forward, folded her hands on the desk blotter. "The workman who came to fix your blinds had a tantrum, and one of our... and a *janitor* stopped him from doing more damage?"

"Yeah, that pretty much covers it."

"But Carl and Wayne both left early today, and Amos is on vacation. That only leaves..." She removed her glasses. "Tell me, what did this janitor look like?"

Aubrey shrugged. "Dark hair and eyes, medium height, an accent—Boston, maybe?—and muscular." She remembered how he'd lifted the bigger, heftier man from his ladder as if he weighed no more than a bed pillow.

"That has to be Franco." She frowned. "But he was told never, ever to enter a patient's room without a staff member." She shook her head. "This puts me in a bit of a quandary. I don't know whether to read him the riot act for breaking the rules, or praise him for coming to your defense."

"A quandary? No disrespect intended, Mrs. Kane, but I don't see the problem. The man deserves a medal. *And* a raise!" She paused. "But... who cleaned up the mess?"

Mrs. Kane stood, walked around the desk, and helped Aubrey to her feet. "I promise to look into it. And the minute I find out, I'll let you know who you can thank."

As the woman guided her to the door, Aubrey was tempted to say, *"Here's your hat, what's your hurry?"* Instead, she said, "No rush, though. That set-to with the contractor took more out of me than I care to admit. I'm going to bed. You can let me know tomorrow, or whenever it works with your schedule."

"Understood. Tomorrow then. Now go," Mrs. Kane said, giving her a gentle shove. "And get a good night's sleep. You really do look like you need it."

Chapter Eight

"DON'T LOOK SO GLUM, FRANCO," MRS. KANE SAID. "YOUR work has been exemplary. In the short while you've been here, you've made quite an impression, and I've heard nothing but good things from staff and residents, and even patients' visitors."

Then why am I here, in your office?

"One resident in particular sang your praises just last evening."

"I was only too happy to help Earl pop on a new wheelchair battery so he could charge the old one."

"No, it wasn't Earl."

Mr. Swenson's daughter, then. She'd collapsed in tears the other day, unable to face the prospect of clearing her recently deceased father's things from his room. So Franco had offered to do it for her; after packing two boxes with the man's final worldly possessions, he'd carried them to her car. When she fell into his arms, crying, thanking him, he'd felt awkward, but it paled by comparison to the blush-inducing feeling that followed her grateful and trembly kiss to the cheek.

He'd rescued See-See when she rolled her weird white wheelchair into a corner and got stuck there, but how would she have reported it when she seemed incapable of verbal communication?

The fact was, he'd done a couple dozen things during his hours at Savannah Falls. If David heard that, he'd probably aggravate his hernia from laughing. Not that he'd blame the guy; thoughtful gestures and acts of kindness weren't exactly synonymous with the name Franco Allessi. If anyone had told him that doing good deeds would make him feel good enough to want to do more of them, *he* probably would have developed a hernia from laughing!

"You've made quite an impression on everyone," she said again, "including me. And believe me when I say it takes a lot more than twenty hours' work to impress the likes of me!"

If she still felt that way after he'd served his final hour, he'd ask her to pass that on to the judge. But since it didn't seem she intended to tell him which resident had been raving about him, he saw no point in dawdling.

"Well, if there isn't anything else," he said, rising, "I told Amos I'd mow the acres over by the gazebo this morning."

"No. That can wait."

He sat back down.

"Tell me about this altercation between a contractor and Mrs. Brewer."

Franco's heart beat a little faster. So, he decided, she'd gone the good news-bad news route without asking which he'd rather hear first.

"Well, the guy was giving her a pretty hard time," he began. "To tell the truth, I would have stayed out of it if he hadn't knocked her bookshelf over." He pictured the woman's big, damp blue eyes, her trembling lower lip, the way she hugged that box of art supplies as if it were a vulnerable infant. He had a name for her now: Mrs. Brewer. "She, ah, she got pretty upset, demanded that both us leave. So we did."

"But not without a bit of a set-to...?"

Franco shrugged. He'd come *this* close to cleaning the guy's clock.

"And the cleanup?"

Franco stared at a loose thread in the carpet between his work boots. "You've got a snag, here," he said, pointing at it, "but you don't want to cut it, or it'll run clear over to the wall."

"Oh?" She stood, leaned forward to peer over the desktop. "Can it be mended?"

Nodding, Franco said, "Sure, with the right supplies. Name a good time, and I'll come back and fix it right up for you." *Couldn't hurt to earn a few brownie points,* he thought. *Especially since she knew full well that he'd entered a patient's room, sans staffer.*

"Wonderful. You can do it just as soon as you've finished the mowing. I have a staff meeting in the conference room that'll last at least through lunchtime." She lifted her key ring, slipped one off and handed it to him. "That'll get you in here, and when you're finished, you can just leave it on my desk. The door will lock automatically behind you."

He turned it over in his hand a few times, marveling that she trusted him to enter her office—alone.

"Now about this cleanup," she continued. "I imagine it took a while to find a Savannah Falls employee to go into Mrs. Brewer's room with you."

"Not really. One of the nurses," he said, "was waiting for her son to pick her up. She wasn't happy about the kid being late, but it gave me time to get everything looking normal again before she… before Mrs. Brewer got back."

"Where did you find the TV and stereo?"

"The nurse told me that nobody ever uses the electronics in the library. So I figured why not put them to good use until—"

He stopped himself, because it seemed cruel, even for a drunken bum like him, to say *"—until she dies."*

"Don't feel bad about not completing the sentence. I've been here for years, and I still have trouble, especially with residents who've been with us a while."

"How long has, ah, Mrs. Brewer been here?"

"A little more than a month." She smiled. "But she has a way of growing on you. Even when common sense tells you it isn't a good idea to get close."

Nodding, he asked, "What kind of cancer?"

"I'm not at liberty to say." She stood again. "Aubrey is very open about her condition, though. So I'm sure if you ask, she'll tell you all about it herself."

Aubrey, he repeated mentally. No point memorizing it, he told himself. He probably wouldn't see her again, and even if he did, it wasn't likely she'd want anything to do with him. Franco stood too, and noticed the blue jay hopping from branch to branch in the red maple just outside her window. It was the same bird. He knew, because he recognized that split in its bright blue crest.

"Thanks," he said, pocketing her key. "Have a good day."

"You too." She came around to the front side of the desk. "You know," she said, crossing her arms over her chest, "when you arrived, I would have sworn you'd put in your hours—a chip on your shoulder the whole time—and nothing more. Thank you for proving me wrong. And thank you for going above and beyond. You've renewed my faith in human nature."

Franco felt the heat of a blush creeping into his face, and hid it by hotfooting it into the hall.

What would David say if he heard that? Something like, "What... did you agree to marry her ugly daughter or something?"

Before coming to Savannah Falls, a crack like that would have made Franco laugh too. Today, for a reason he couldn't explain, it didn't seem the least bit funny.

Because it felt good, real good, having people see him as a decent guy for a change.

Chapter Nine

"MY ADVICE, AUBREY," MRS. KANE SAID, "IS THAT YOU make yourself a little less conspicuous."

Aubrey looked up from her sketch pad. "Excuse me?"

"Sketches, notes, intense stares from afar... I'm surprised *Franco* hasn't noticed."

Aubrey closed her sketchbook, slid the charcoal pencil into its spiral binding, and giggled quietly. "Didn't realize I was being so obvious."

"Well, to be honest, you weren't. I might not have noticed at all if your mother hadn't called my attention to it."

"My mother?" Aubrey looked around. "She's here?"

"She stopped by my office yesterday, on her way out. She believes he must be a gigolo or a charlatan, moving in on you at the most vulnerable point in your life." Mrs. Kane pointed at the sketchbook. "Said you've always been a feet-on-the-ground, level-headed woman, but that ever since—and I quote, 'Ever since *that man* came onto the scene,' you're distant and moody, and all you want to do is work on capturing his likeness on canvas."

Aubrey sighed. "Good ol' Mama," she said. "Never crossed her mind, did it, that maybe, just maybe, my behavior has more do with the fact that I've been coping with a death sentence for months. Or the Arbitral I take to control the tremors. But a crush on the hospice handyman? I don't know whether to laugh or cry." She shook her head. "If I live to be a hundred, I'll never understand what makes that woman tick." Then she laughed. "Oh. Wait. I can't live to be a hundred, now can I?"

Mrs. Kane winced. "And if *I* live to be a hundred, I'll never get used to the way you people cope with your prognoses."

"Whatever works, though, because the patient is always right, right?"

"I suppose."

"So what can you tell me about this mysterious Franco Allessi? I mean, if I'm going to leave him all my worldly possessions, I should know *something* about him. Such as... where did he live before moving to Georgia? I'm guessing Rhode Island. Massachusetts, even, based on his accent. And what sort of work did he do before coming to Savannah Falls?"

"Now, now, Aubrey, how fair would it be if I answered your questions? I'm prohibited from releasing any information about you to Mr. Allessi, so..."

"But what if he's a serial purse snatcher, a cat burglar, a diamond smuggler? That isn't very fair, putting a man like that into my path." Aubrey squinted one eye. "Wait just a minute here. Did you just imply that he came to you, to talk about *me*?"

Laughing, Mrs. Kane said, "You've been reading way too many James Patterson novels. Trust me, Franco is as harmless as a bunny. Hardly as dangerous—or interesting—as a once-upon-a-time criminal." She sobered slightly to add, "After you told me how he came to your defense with the contractor, I had a talk with him. We won't be using that company any more, by the way, so there's no need to worry you'll ever see that man again."

Remembering Mrs. Kane's discomfort with dark humor, she resisted the urge to say another meeting between her and the angry man wasn't likely, since *she'd* likely not last until his next visit. Instead, she followed the flight path of the blue jay that so often chattered at her from outside her window. It landed in a cedar tree, mere feet from where Franco was busy trimming dead branches near the trunk.

"He's very good with things that grow, isn't he?"

"Yes, he is. This much I *can* tell you about Franco: he and his wife once owned a landscaping company."

"Once owned? Did the company go belly-up, or did he lose her to divorce? Not both, I hope."

"She was killed in a car accident," Mrs. Kane finished.

And Franco had been in the car. Aubrey would have bet her short life on it. The fact that he'd survived when his wife hadn't, well, that went a long way in explaining his tendency to sometimes stare into the distance, especially while tending the roses. At least, that's how she saw things…

Aubrey opened the sketchbook and knew in a glance what was wrong with her sketch of Franco. She packed up her things. "Thanks, Mrs. Kane. You've been a big help."

"I was? Well, all right then, you're welcome!"

The eyes, Aubrey realized, making her way to the elevator. The missing piece of the puzzle would fall into place just as soon as she figured out how to capture that *look* in his eyes.

Chapter Ten

AUBREY BREWER HAD LEFT THE PACKAGE WITH MRS. Kane, but Franco didn't want to open it there in her office. He took it home, instead, and sat on the loveseat to savor the moment. It had been a long, long time since anyone had given him a gift.

He read the card first:

Dear Mr. Alessi,

Thank you for your help last week. It's nice to know that chivalry isn't dead.

Fondly,
Aubrey Brewer

Smiling, he slid the card back into its envelope, taking care to put it down far from paper plates bearing pizza crusts or half-eaten sandwiches. He slid his fingertips across the wrapping paper, yellow roses on a white background. How could she have known that—because they were Jill's favorite, they'd become his favorite too?

Slowly, carefully, he peeled back the paper. A quiet chuckle popped from his lips. "Well, I'll be," he said aloud. "It's a painting. A painting of *me*."

Franco carried it to the window, to inspect it under a shaft of afternoon light. She'd placed him in the front garden at Savannah Falls, standing waist-deep in yellow floribunda. The detail was amazing, from blue-gray shadows that fell between the folds of his cuffed sleeves to the lines crossing the palm that cradled a single rosebud, cupped in his palm. She'd painted his eyes in such a way that he wasn't looking at the bloom. Rather, she'd aimed his gaze up and forward, so that it seemed he was looking into a mirror.

"I fall in love with you all over again," Jill used to say, "when you look at me like that."

"Like what?" he'd ask, every time. She'd tried hard to find the right words so he'd know. But those words never materialized, and he hadn't understood.

Until now, Franco thought, staring at the painting.

The one-bedroom house trailer he'd bought soon after she died had come furnished, and included a small, faux-stone fireplace that stood against the far wall. With the flip of a switch, a tiny fan whirred above a clear-red lightbulb. He hated the manufacturer's half-baked attempt to duplicate flickering flames, and would have taken the thing to the dump... if he could've mustered the energy to get the job done. So he'd put the fake wood mantel to use, holding twin oil lanterns that he lit when the power went out. Above them, the picture he'd taken of Jill on their twentieth anniversary—two weeks to the day before she died. It had always bothered him that her image hung there, off-center, looking toward the windowless back wall. If he put Mrs. Brewer's painting to its left, it would seem as though Jill was looking at *him* again.

He left it on the sofa, right beside her sweet thank-you note. Franco found his hammer, drove a nail into the imitation knotty pine paneling, and hung the painting beside Jill's photo.

Then he sat down to admire his handiwork, and Mrs. Brewer's amazing talent. It didn't seem right that anything so thoughtful should be surrounded by empty soda cans, fast food wrappers, and Ho-Ho boxes. He grabbed a trash bag and filled it. Filled a second, and carried both to the dented aluminum can that he stored under his tiny back porch. A few swipes of the vacuum cleaner, a couple passes with a Pledge-soaked rag, and the living room made the kitchen look like a junkyard by comparison. So he cleared the table of coffee mugs and balled-up napkins, washed the dishes, and put them away. He tackled the bedroom next, and the bathroom, the front porch, and the back deck. For the first time since unpacking his suitcase here, the place was white-glove clean, all because Aubrey Brewer had decided—for some unknown reason—to give him a watercolor painting that made him look as good as Mrs. Kane's compliments had made him feel.

He didn't think it was possible to thank her for that, but he aimed to try.

The next day, he made a point of dragging the big trash can past her room, but she wasn't there. Half an hour later, he checked again, but she still hadn't returned. Franco began to worry that something might have happened to her. Something… permanent. His heart sank, and he felt weak in the knees. She was a stranger. He didn't even remember her first name! They'd said hello and nodded politely when passing one another in the hall. Once, in the few minutes it took to get from the lobby to the third floor, they'd commented on the weather without taking their eyes off the glowing digits above the doors. How could she have touched him so intensely in such a short time? What he felt for her wasn't pity. It wasn't sexual or romantic. But it was real, and it was deep, and it confused the hell out of him.

He should have done more for her the other day. Should have gone into her room *before* that idiot had a chance to break the knickknacks and keepsakes that had meant enough to her that she'd surrounded herself with them here, in the place she'd come to die. *Why* hadn't he done more? Because, as usual, he'd been thinking of himself, worrying that if he went into her room, Mrs. Kane would kick him to the curb and he'd have to start his fifty hours all over again, doing only God knew what, God knew where.

And now? *Now?* Now she was gone and he hadn't even had a chance to thank her for the hours she'd spent on the painting. Didn't have a chance to say goodbye.

The elevator doors opened, hissed shut, and the sound of flip-flops echoed in the wide, polished tile hallway. She'd been wearing flip-flops that day as she crouched on the floor, hugging the art kit to her chest. Flip-flops with little white daisies that rested gently on her toes. He remembered because it had seemed odd that a woman who'd matched skirts and scarves to the colors in the sandals wasn't wearing polish on her toes, as Jill always had.

Franco was almost afraid to turn around and find someone else walking around in those sole-slapping shoes, someone who wasn't—

"You're a hard man to find," she said. "I've been looking everywhere for you."

Heart hammering, Franco grinned, and shaking with relief, said, "Ditto…"

Chapter Eleven

"HERE," SHE SAID, "HOLD THESE WHILE I OPEN THE door."

"Say, is this the guy with the Afro who paints faster than I blink?"

Grinning, she said, "One and the same. They're Bob Ross DVDs. I don't know which I like better, his paintings or his soft, soothing voice."

"'And a happy little tree lives right here,'" they said at the same time.

Chuckling, he said, "You look better today."

"Thanks," she said, tossing her things on the foot of her bed. "Confession time: I asked Mrs. Kane about you, but she wouldn't say a word. Not even when I tried trick questions, such as, is he a bank robber or escapee from an insane asylum?" Shaking her head, Aubrey grinned. "The woman is a living, breathing Fort Knox where information is concerned, I tell you."

She looked at him, standing with one hand on the door jamb, the other on the handle of his oversized trash receptacle, toes carefully on the *outside* of her threshold.

"Didn't your mother teach you it's impolite to stand in an open doorway, letting all the air conditioning out?"

The entire facility was climate controlled, and from the look on her face, he realized she already knew that. To her credit, she didn't comment. Instead, she laughed, and the sound of it was easy on his ears.

"I like your laugh," she said. "Nothing like my ex—loud, raucous, spewed out for the sole purpose of getting attention. Or, if he'd already gained it, to ensure he held onto his precious center-stage spot."

Franco had never met the guy and hoped he never would.

"Look, I know the rules," she told him. "And I also know that *you* know the rules. But this place doesn't come cheap—just ask my mother—and if I want to—"

"Ask me what, Bree?"

Agnes pushed past Franco and into her daughter's room.

Oh great, just what I need... president of the Optimist Club.

Aubrey's smile looked forced, and he couldn't blame her.

"I was just explaining to Mr. Allessi, here, the high cost of kicking the bucket in a place like this. And that I think it's ridiculous that—given the inflated price tag—I can't invite a person into my room unless he's chewing on a silver spoon... filled with caviar... while being escorted by one of the staff."

Agnes sighed and rolled her eyes. "Honestly, Bree. Stop behaving like a spoiled brat. It's very unbecoming."

She faced Franco. Eyes narrowed, she said, "Is there something we can do for you?"

Her daughter had already been through enough, and he wasn't about to add to her misery. He held up the DVDs, toes still carefully placed behind the invisible "do not cross" line.

"I, ah, your daughter... Mrs. Brewer," he began, "asked me to hold these while she carried some things into her room."

"Well, she seems nicely settled now, so..."

Aubrey sighed, and Agnes snatched the DVDs from Franco's hand. "*Do* feel free to get back to your—" She glanced at the collection, then looked at her daughter. "Seriously, Bree? If you're going to spend what little is left of your hard-earned money and dwindling hours on earth watching how-to tapes, why not a *respected* artist? Picasso. Rembrandt. Van Gogh?"

Aubrey tapped her chin. "Not a bad idea. But where will I find a collection of *Dead Painters How-to*?"

Agnes aimed a steely glare in Franco's direction. "As I was saying, please don't let us keep you from your work."

He ignored her dismissive tone and focused on Aubrey. "It's good to see that you're feeling a little better," he said, and left the room.

"He's a *janitor*, Bree," he heard the mother say.

Franco made it all the way to the other end of the hall, then stopped. "Even with your squeaky, wobbling wheels," he told the trash can, "you can't drown out the voice of disapproval."

If he'd known just *how* disapproving, Franco might have walked faster. He'd never put a lot of stock in others' opinions of him, but for a reason he couldn't explain, Agnes' words hit him like a sucker punch.

***

"You can be really mean, Mama. And loud, too."

"Please. He's at the other end of the hall by now, pushing that smelly, noisy cart. He didn't hear a thing." She sniffed. "But even if he had, you know what they say…"

"What?"

"The truth hurts."

In her condition, this could be their last conversation, and Aubrey didn't want her mother living with the guilt of hard words between them to haunt her. She relieved her mother of the DVDs and eased into her recliner. "You have no idea how many people have come to appreciate art because of this man," she said, holding up the packages, "and how many more have tried their hand at painting because of his gentle teaching techniques. He *is* a respected painter, and you know what else? *He died of cancer.* So I have more in common, lots more in common, with him than any artist you can name!"

A wave of nausea and lightheadedness rolled over her. If she wasn't already seated, Aubrey sensed she would have crumpled, like a marionette whose puppeteer had let go of the strings.

Agnes bent at the waist. "Aubrey? What's wrong? You're white as a bedsheet. Shall I call a nurse?"

She waved off her mother's concern. "I'm fine. Just a little woozy. It's the—" Aubrey bit her lower lip. If her mother found out she was taking meds to control the tremors instead of chemotherapy and pain pills, she'd pitch a fit. It might be an exercise in futility, but Aubrey had made up her mind: she had no control over the cancer, how fast it spread, or the time and place it would end her life, but she *did* have a say in how she'd spend her final days. Painting gave her a respite from pain, from thinking about death, and she couldn't do it with shaky hands.

"Aubrey, I declare. Sometimes you make me feel so blasted *helpless.*" Head down and elbows cupped, Agnes began pacing. "If only I knew what I could do for you!"

"You can apologize to Mr. Allessi, for starters."

"Apologize? For *what*?"

"For every insulting thing you've said, and implied."

"Such as...?"

"Such as he's only showing an interest in me in the hope I'll put him in my will. If I told him that I've exhausted my savings and investments, that the few dollars left in my trust are what's paying for this place—this place *you* insisted on—nothing would change. He works here, Mama. His only interest in me is as a Savannah Falls patient."

"That isn't entirely true," Franco said.

She whirled around and faced the door. "What are you, part cat?" Aubrey asked him. "How long have you been standing there?"

"Long enough." He faced Agnes. "I'm giving you the benefit of the doubt, thinking your behavior is motivated by maternal concern. But she's right. I have *no* personal interest in her *or* her money. So here's an idea: stop trying to control her every breath. Just be her mom, and enjoy every minute she has left. If you don't, you'll regret it for the rest of *your* life."

Spoken like a man with his own regrets, Aubrey thought.

Then, hands up like a man being held at gunpoint, Franco shook his head and made his way back down the hall.

Neither mother nor daughter spoke until the sound of plastic wheels faded.

"How dare he speak to me that way! Why, he's nothing but—"

"Nothing but *right.*"

"Right? Right about what?"

Aubrey held out her hand, willed her mother to take it. "Just be my mom, okay? For as long as you can."

The hum and whir of a motorized wheelchair interrupted them.

"You two auditioning for a Hallmark greeting card commercial?" Dusty called out.

"What's he babbling about?" Agnes whispered.

"He's referring to the beautiful mother-daughter moment he just witnessed," Aubrey said. "Go back to your room, little brat," she said, waving him on.

Dusty tipped his hat and started rolling forward. "See you soon, genius… if neither of us croaks in the next couple hours."

Aubrey's head was pounding, and the lightheadedness had become a full-blown dizzy spell. She leaned forward and, rubbing her temples, said, "Mama, I hate to be rude—although apparently it's programmed into my DNA—but I need to lie down."

"I'm sorry if I upset you, Bree." She perched on the chair's arm. "That certainly wasn't my intention." Sliding an arm across Aubrey's shoulders, she drew her into a sideways hug. "It's just that I can't bear to see you hurt by some swindler."

Swindler, indeed, Aubrey thought.

Agnes crossed the room, picked up her purse and added, "I love you, you know. Promise me that if that awful janitor comes back again, you'll call security."

Eyes shut tight, she said, "Love you too, Mama."

Tomorrow, she'd find Franco and apologize for the things her mother had said. But tonight, she'd say a little prayer... that the "awful man" *would* come back. He'd barged into her room— into her life—and fought for her with no thought to what it might cost him. That's the stuff real friends were made of, she decided.

She had dozens of acquaintances, and her mother loved her in her clumsy, controlling way. But friends? Aubrey's life was seriously lacking in that department right now.

And nobody should die without at least *one* friend to miss her.

Chapter Twelve

DAVID SHOOK HIS HEAD. "BUMMER, MAN. BUT LOOK AT the bright side. Maybe the woman is auditioning for Mama Lion poster girl."

"Yeah, well, just eighteen hours to go, y'know? I can put up with just about anything for that long."

"So it's going pretty good over there, huh?"

"It's going great, actually. I was in danger of getting flabby, driving Clayton's tow truck." Franco patted his belly. "This job has been good for me in more ways than one."

"Talked with Krissi yesterday," David said. "Said she's gonna be real sorry to see you leave."

"Krissi?"

"Mrs. Kane." David chuckled. "You might want to see a doctor, pal."

Franco braced himself for a wisecrack.

"Yeah, a proctologist... to get your head outta yer butt. You've been there two weeks and you don't know her first name?"

"I thought it was Kristine." Shrugging, he picked up the catsup bottle, gave its bottom a whack. "Nicknames never came up during routine conversations. Besides, I didn't see much point in getting all cozy with people I'll never see again."

"I wouldn't be so sure about that if I were you." Grimacing at the growing mound of red, David said, "Would you like some fries to go with your catsup? Jeez, bud, leave some for the rest of us!"

"Sorry." Sorry… Franco would bet his trailer that he'd said that word more since taking the job at Savannah Falls than at any other time in his life. For waking sleeping patients with noise from the trash cart. For emptying a wheelbarrow full of dried leaves too near the compost pile. For letting the wind catch the shed door and slam it behind him.

"So this Brewster woman who's got you all tied up in knots… what's her story?"

"Brewer. Aubrey Brewer. Not sure what type of cancer she has, but she's an artist, and from what I saw, a pretty good one. And she's divorced. Sounds like the guy was a jerk. But me? Tied up in knots over her? I'd hardly put it that way. At least, not for the reasons you think."

"Well, whatever the reasons, just be careful. You've barely climbed back onto the wagon. I'd hate to see you fall off again because you went all loopy over some woman who's about to die." David cringed. "Now *I'm* sorry. And you're right. I *am* tactless sometimes."

"Sometimes?" Franco chuckled. "But you digress. You said you and, uh, and *Krissi* had a talk about me?"

"Oh. Right. That." David crunched into his pickle. "She swore me to secrecy, so when she pops the question, you have to play dumb."

"Playing dumb. Ha! That'll be a piece of cake. But wait… isn't Mrs. Kane already married?"

"Real funny, Allessi. Not *that* question. The 'come to work for me full time' question."

Franco stopped chewing and sputtered, "Wh-what?"

"You heard right. She likes your work. She likes the way you interact with people—though I gotta admit, that one baffled me—and she likes *you*." He sipped his coffee. "Would you believe that she actually said everyone else who has come into contact with you feels the same way?"

"Hmpf. Evidently, neither you nor Krissi have spoken with the blue jay."

"The…" David's brow furrowed. "The *what?*"

Franco gave a couple examples of how the blue jay had been his flighty shadow since he'd first set foot on the Savannah Falls property.

David stared at him for a minute. "Stalked by a bird." He shook his head. "Leave it to you."

"I swear. It's true. Every word."

"Yeah, well, anyway, it might be a good idea to have an answer ready, so you won't look like a boob when Krissy presents the idea. Something that'll keep her thinking you're the next best thing to sliced bread while she's writing up her report for the judge."

"Quit pullin' my leg," Franco said, smirking. "I can't work off the last of my hours if I'm limping."

"Oh, you're on a roll today, aren't you? I know a guy who does standup comedy down at the Wormhole. Want me to put in a good word for you? You know, in case you can't decide between swabbin' the johns over at Clayton's garage and pullin' weeds at the hospice?"

Most times, he liked David's tell-it-like-it-is tendencies. But once in a while…

He was flattered to hear that Mrs. Kane had spoken so highly of him. Franco loved the work. Didn't even mind cleaning bathrooms… much. But to stay on, permanently? He'd have to give that some thought. A whole lot of thought.

As David drove toward the trailer, the conversation turned to sports, the weather, David's wife and kids. And when he pulled into the parking pad beside the porch, he whistled.

"Whoa. What happened here?"

Franco got out of the pickup truck and leaned back in to say, "Aw, gimme a break. I clean up once in a while."

"Hey, every three years is better than never. But the inside is still a sty, right?"

"Fat lot you know. It'd pass my Marine drill sergeant's inspection."

David shut down the motor and followed Franco to the porch. "Yeah? Well, I'll believe it when I see it."

After stepping into the living room, he whistled again. "Wait. I know what's going on here. You met some cute li'l nurse over at Savannah Falls, and *she* did all this for you."

"Much as I like the idea of a cute li'l nurse pampering me..."

"Seriously." David met his eyes. "You did this."

"Believe it or not, this neat 'n tidy stuff is habit-forming."

Walking up to the fireplace, David pointed. "Did your Mrs. Brewer paint that?"

"She isn't mine, but yeah. It's a thank-you gift, for rescuing her from a bully." Franco gave him a quick rundown of what had happened.

Hands clasped over his chest, David sighed. "Be still my heart," he said in a squeaky tenor. Then, "You sure that's a good idea? I hate to repeat myself, and I don't mean to sound cruel, but she's gonna check out soon. What happens to *you*, afterward?"

Franco groaned. "How many times do I have to tell you, it isn't like that between us."

Eyes on the portrait again, David said, "Coulda fooled me." Then, one eyebrow cocked, he added, "But c'mon. Something's going on. How else do you explain that *look* on your face?"

In all honesty, he couldn't explain it. And since he was in no mood to tell the whole *"Jill said I looked at her that way"* story, Franco spoke in a falsetto voice, too: "Well, I have laundry and dishes to do, so if you'll excuse me..."

Laughing, David moved toward the door, firing a playful punch to Franco's shoulder on the way. "I gotta tell ya, dude, it does my old heart good to see you pulling your act together this way. I hope for your sake it lasts this time."

After his "nothing's going on" talk, the last thing Franco wanted was for his sponsor to catch him returning to Savannah Falls after hours. So he killed time, waiting for David to drive away, and getting online to investigate how to go about becoming a CPA, like David. The guy was forever complaining that he couldn't keep up with clients' accounting needs. But Franco had never heard him gripe about the big house, the status car, or the cost of tuition for his kids' private schools. Franco had dropped out of college after earning sixty credits— almost enough for an Associate's degree. Add a hundred hours and $20,000—give or take a couple grand— and voila, a license to practice numbers.

"Idiot," he grumbled to himself, "who are you fooling? You don't even like math."

An ad for Burpee Seeds appeared in his search engine's sidebar, and with it, photos of what the plants would become— in time and with the proper care. Half of his former customers had *become* his customers in the first place because they had no idea what to do once the sprouts appeared. He and Jill had started "Leafit to Us" on a whim and a shoestring, and within five years had built it into the number-two landscape company in the Manchester area, with thousands of customers and nearly a hundred employees. They'd done it on their own, without bank loans or investors... or college degrees.

He powered down the laptop and grabbed his jacket and, locking the door behind him, decided it made no sense to build a new mousetrap. During the half-mile walk to the hospice center, he considered the start-up costs: Apply for a commercial license. Line up some insurance. Hire a lawyer to draw up a service contract. Buy some equipment and a shed to store it in. Thirty customers, minimum, he estimated, would keep his head above water, and to find them, he'd need business cards, magnetic signs for the Jeep, maybe even a website. Ten grand, he figured, would get him up and running, but with his lousy credit, he'd have to work for it and save it. That meant sticking with Clayton full time, and maintaining clients' properties, evenings and weekends, alone. Unless *Krissy* could offer more hours and a better salary...

The big white mansion came into view. Who would've thought, a few weeks ago, that a place like this would change him in every conceivable way?

In the past, he'd made a dozen half-baked stabs at sobriety, at cleaning up his act. But as David had so often pointed out, it takes grit and guts to fight temptation—and win. "Once a Marine, always a Marine, right? So quit feeling sorry for yourself; soldier on and find the missing puzzle piece."

But he'd lived so long in a fog of guilt, shame, and loneliness that he had no idea how to look for some mysterious, metaphorical puzzle piece.

It had taken Savannah Falls to help him find it: hope, and the slow-dawning awareness that a spark of decency had survived the self-centered, sometimes-depraved way he'd lived his life. For the first time in a long time, he believed in himself, *liked* the man he was becoming.

"Thank you, Judge Malloy," he said, chuckling as he climbed the steps.

"Talking to yourself again?"

"Dusty. Hey, bud. What's up?"

"Oh, I dunno, Mr. Original. The sky? Boogers in your nose?" Franco chose to ignore the juvenile wisecrack.

"So how'd you get so special, anyway, coming and going when you please?" Dusty smirked. "Oh. Wait. I'll bet I know. You're gettin' it on with Mrs. Kane, aren't ya?"

"Not only is that flat-out rude, it's a boldfaced lie. You'd best watch what you say or—"

"Or what," Dusty interrupted. "You're a *janitor*. You can't tell me what to do."

He felt bad for the kid. It couldn't be easy, hearing that your life was almost over even before it even had a chance to fully begin. If he'd had kids, Franco hoped he'd raise them up right, as his grandfather used to say, and teach them the importance of respect—for yourself and for others—no matter what. It was a lesson he'd forgotten, until the hospice gave him a dose of be-thankful-for-what-you-have reality. He felt sorry for Dusty, too, because his loved ones were so afraid of losing him that they didn't realize that by molly-coddling him, they were depriving him of the serenity and pride that comes from knowing you've done your best, given your all, even in the face of terrifying, insurmountable odds... maybe even *because* of it.

"I prefer the term *custodian*, if you don't mind. But you make a good point. I can't tell you what to do."

Dusty pecked something into his paperback-sized tablet.

"But here's what I *can* do." Franco squatted, making himself eye level with the boy. "I can tell you that everybody in this place is grappling with the same god-awful prognosis that you are." He paused, and when he saw that he had the boy's attention, added, "And I can tell you that I've been all through this big old place, heard people cry out in pain and wail at the unfairness of it all. So can the 'poor, poor, pitiful me' junk. You're better than that. Smarter than that. Show some respect to the staff—don't worry, I'm a volunteer, so you can still mouth off to me—and to your family. Because this isn't easy on them either, you know."

Dusty leaned back slightly, eyebrows high on his forehead, clearly surprised.

Franco said, "Well?"

"Well what?"

"You gonna ease up on folks around here?" Dusty shrugged.

"You gonna at least try?"

Another shrug, and then, "'Do or do not. There is no *try.*'"

"Yoda would be proud." Franco stood. "You look cold. What are you doing out here in this wind?"

"They're cleaning my room, and I'm not allowed in there until they're finished." He made a half-baked attempt at a grin. "Haven't you heard? Cleaning products can kill ya."

"Now that you mention it, yeah, I think I did read something like that." He shook his head. "How 'bout if I move you into the lobby, get you in out of this wind?"

"No thanks."

As the hospice's youngest patient, Dusty had probably tired of hearing "poor kid," "isn't it a shame," and "so sad, he's so young." In his shoes, Franco would avoid people every chance he got, too. So he shrugged out of his jacket and draped it around the boy's shoulders.

"Goodwill, or Salvation Army store?" Dusty asked, grinning like the Cheshire cat.

"Shows what *you* know about men's fashion. Just so happens this was purchased during a K-Mart blue-light special."

"By your great-great-grandfather? Because it's special, all right. And old." He looked up at Franco... and *laughed.*

"I'm gonna buy myself a hot chocolate from the vending machine. Should I make it two?"

"Nah." He pointed at the shiny red can on the railing. "But thanks."

Franco set the timer on his cell phone. "I'll be back in ten minutes. If you're still out here in this squall, I'm taking you inside, no matter what you say. Got it?"

"Better check with Mrs. Kane first. I don't think coddling patients is in your job description."

In the lobby, Franco ran into Jake McGillivray—and no fewer than a dozen of his friends and relatives. Their laughing and joking irked some patients and their visitors, but Franco thought the happy mayhem lent a good balance to the usually somber and hushed halls. Today, in place of brownies, cookies, or lemon bars, they passed a plate of fudge around. When Jake spotted Franco, he waved him over. "Have some, kid, it'll put hair on your chest!"

"Too late for that," he said, helping himself to a piece.

Jake had arrived the day after Franco, and as he'd helped Mrs. McGillivray carry personal items into Jake's room, she'd explained that his multiple myeloma was causing him to "… fall apart from the inside out." She'd seen a lot of mule-headed stubbornness in their fifty-two years together, she'd added, but his refusal to take the prescribed opiates "just takes the cake, especially when something as simple as rolling over in bed could fracture a bone. I'm tired of watching him suffer, and *that* is why he's here."

Maybe the staff had convinced Jake to take his medicine, because he sure didn't appear to be suffering now!

"Well, what do you think?" Jake asked. "Is it the best thing that ever passed your lips?"

"It's delicious, all right," he agreed, using the uneaten portion of the square to toast Mrs. McGillivray.

Despite her cheery laugh, she looked nearly as peaked as Jake. In some ways, Franco envied her a little, having this time to adjust to lonely nights and strangely long days without her mate. He'd lost Jill in a nanosecond.

He accepted a second piece of the candy and made his way to the third floor. But Aubrey—the only reason he'd come back to the hospice this afternoon—wasn't in her room. Franco wandered the halls looking for her. In Dusty's room. In the library and the sun-room. Even in the dining hall. As he traveled from place to place, residents and their families called, "Hi, Franco!" and "How goes it!" So maybe David hadn't been bluffing when he shared what Mrs. Kane had told him. Franco liked seeing and hearing evidence that he'd made a good impression on so many people in such a short time. If, on day one, anyone had told him he'd come to feel that he belonged here, he would have called them crazy. But he *did* like it here. Liked the job and his coworkers, liked the frail, vulnerable people who'd entrusted the staff with their life moments… himself, included.

That, he thought, *is the other side of the proverbial coin.* He'd been there long enough to have memorized patient names and recognize family members. Even the newest ones. He knew who liked to gab when he passed them in the halls, and who'd rather be left alone to think their own thoughts. Who preferred their trash bags loose in the waste-basket, and who liked them tied down with a nice tight knot. And that, he decided, was the other side of the proverbial coin: getting to know them meant sharing the family's grief—even if only a little bit—when they died.

He'd cleaned and prepped the rooms of five patients who had passed away—two who went peacefully in their sleep, and three who clung on, fighting for every breath, right up until the bitter end. If he worked here full time, could he handle those goodbyes, day in and day out?

"You never really get used to it," Mrs. Kane had said, "but you learn to accept it, for the benefit of the patient and the next—and the one after that—and their loved ones."

The doctors, the nurses, and Mrs. Kane had all studied the process of dying, the phases of grief. Franco had not. These past twenty hours, he'd operated strictly on instinct, talking when it seemed the right thing to do, shutting up when it didn't. If he stayed, would that be enough?

Franco honestly didn't know.

By now, he'd made his way to the solarium, where Jake was once again surrounded by family. They bid the feeble old guy a long and loving goodbye—it was how everyone said goodbye here, since every departure could be the last—then included Franco in the circle of smiles, hugs, and warm words.

"Daddy thinks so much of you," Jake's daughter said. "Thank you for looking out for him, and for making him laugh."

Franco accepted her hug, knowing it was motivated by the knowledge that with every breath, her father moved closer to life's end, and every kindness, however small, was greatly appreciated. And it made him appreciate his own life all the more.

"You're lookin' mighty glum all of a sudden," Jake said once they'd gone.

"Must be the weather."

"Aw, a little rain shouldn't dampen your spirits. It makes things grow. Fella like you, with a talent for plants, oughta love gray skies." He winked. "But you're not fooling *this* old newsman, Franco Allessi. Something is eating at you." He patted the seat beside his wheelchair. "Take a load off. Spill your guts. Tell it like it is." Jake slapped his knee. "Hot *dang* it feels good to spout clichés and not have some *Chicago Manual of Style*-loving editor blue-pencil 'em!"

The comment must have awoken memories, for Jake began talking about his years as a journalist, which had taken him to places like Vietnam, Colombia, and South Africa, and his last assignment in Mogadishu. When he said he'd lived a full, long life, Franco believed him. *A man like that shouldn't go out because of a thing like cancer.*

"Okay, son. Your turn."

"I, ah…"

Jake tapped his temple. "My reporter's brain tells me your story is more interesting than mine."

"Hate to disappoint," Franco said, "but except for a battle with the bottle, my life has been pretty uneventful."

"I'm not buyin' it."

No disrespect intended, Franco thought, *but I'm not interested in dredging up the past.*

"Look at it this way. I'm like a priest, only instead of being protected by vows, you've got the Grim Reaper guaranteeing my confidentiality."

"It isn't that I don't trust you, Jake. It's just, well, there isn't much to tell. I'm not kidding when I say my life has been pretty humdrum to this point." If he had worked harder at finding Aubrey, he'd be with her now, instead of sitting here jawing with Jake. *Just humor the old guy,* he thought. Maybe then the powers that be would reward him with some idea how to find her.

"I was married. Twenty years. But my wife died in a car accident. Young, inexperienced driver T-boned the car."

"Was she alone?"

Franco winced. "No. I was in the passenger seat."

Jake winced too. "Damn. That's rough. Sorry, Franco."

"Soon as I got out of the hospital, I started drinking. Eventually, I lost our house and the landscaping business, and ended up driving a tow truck."

"Ah. Now I get it. You're here serving out a community service sentence, are ya?"

There wasn't much point in denying it. "Fifty hours."

"Must've been Judge Malloy."

Just as Franco about to say "How'd you know?," Jake continued, "Had my own run-in with the blowhard, decade or so ago. And put in my time with Jimmy Carter and one of his Habitat for Humanity projects." He pulled up his sleeve, showed Franco the rope-like scar that ran the length of his forearm. "Would've rolled off the roof if a nail hadn't slowed me down."

Franco winced. "Whoa. That's some story."

Jake chuckled and pulled the sleeve down again. "Got me out of the last three hours of community service, too."

"Wow," Franco said. "Just, wow."

"One more question, kid."

Kid? Franco stifled a laugh. He was almost old enough to be Aubrey's dad! Then it dawned on him that Jake hadn't finished his inquisition just yet. Franco could save the guy a lot of time by admitting he'd pretty much wiped the "My Past Life" board clean with his abbreviated confession. There really wasn't much more to know about him, but he went along with the guy.

"So," Franco said, rubbing his palms together, "what would you like to know?"

"Why are you still sitting here, staring at my ugly old mug, when it's plain as the nose on your face that you'd rather be with Aubrey?"

Chapter Thirteen

AUBREY HAD WATCHED ONE EPISODE OF *THE JOY OF Painting* and felt pretty good about the fall-inspired mountainscape she'd created. Still, it lacked something, something she couldn't quite define.

She clamped the canvas on the easel, packed up her oil paints and, after filling a cup with paint cleaner, left her brushes soaking in the bathroom.

A quiet knock on the door jamb, followed by, "That's too good to hide away in your room."

"Franco!" Smiling, Aubrey added, "You don't mind my using your first name, do you?"

"Not at all… Aubrey."

"Can you come in?"

"I'm not sure. When I'm on duty, it's against regs. I'm not on duty right now, but you're still a patient and I'm still a sorta employee, so…" Shoulders raised, he extended both hands, palms up.

"Let's play it safe, then, and go right to the source for the answer." She stepped into the hall and pulled the door shut. "I only close it when I'm going to be out for more than a few minutes. And at night, of course. And just to ease your mind, I have it on good authority that Mrs. Kane will be in her office, going over some files."

"On a Sunday?"

"On a Sunday." She led the way toward the elevators. "Amazing, isn't it, that in this day and age, when everyone is looking for shortcuts and ways to avoid work, everyone working here is just that dedicated. And none more than the Savannah Falls Hospice director."

He punched the "down" button.

"I have to warn you, though, this little jaunt of ours might take a while. My gait is shorter and more sluggish than it used to be before... you know."

"It's good to take things slow sometimes. Besides, I didn't know you in your fast-and-giant-steps days, so I'll have nothing to compare it—"

"Ah, you're a 'take time to smell the roses' man, are you?"

"I've never been a 'smell the roses' guy. But there's a first time for everything."

He was taller and more broad-shouldered than she remembered. Was it the crisp white shirt that made his hair and eyes look darker? Maybe those dim curlicue light bulbs in her room were to blame for the image she'd stored in her memory. Aubrey made a mental note to ask for replacements, then realized Franco was probably just the person to ask.

"Would you happen to know how I might get my hands on some of those energy-efficient light bulbs? You know... the ones that power up brighter than incandescents or those ridiculous swirly things?"

"I, ah, I can look into it for you."

The elevator doors opened and, hand extended, he made sure they couldn't close before she'd stepped into the car. He might be a bit rough around the edges, but Franco hadn't forgotten how to behave like a gentleman.

"Need more light for when you paint at night, huh?"

"Something like that," she said, echoing his earlier reply. Standing this close to him, looking into those dark-lashed brown eyes, Aubrey had to smile. Yes, she'd captured his overall mood and look fairly well, if she did say so herself.

"Speaking of painting," he said as the doors opened to the lobby floor, "I've been carrying this around for days, trying to get it to you."

Franco held up a package, wrapped in the same paper she'd used for his portrait.

"Oh my," she said, hands clasped under her chin, "for me?"

He tipped the package, so she could read the card. AUBREY BREWER, it said. And it was underlined. Twice.

"I *love* surprises. But would you mind holding on to it until after we've talked with Mrs. Kane?"

"Sure," he said, tucking it back under his arm. "No problem."

"What's that sly smile all about?"

"Nothing. Just... did you know that Mrs. Kane's first name is Krissi?"

Aubrey blinked. "Now that you mention it, the name plate on her desk says Kristine. But I've never referred to her that way. Never called her Krissi, either, for that matter."

"Krissi doesn't really fit her 'do it by the book, all business' personality, does it?"

"No, it certainly doesn't." Aubrey giggled. "What do you bet she was a chess champ in high school?"

"President of her class."

"Editor of the school newspaper."

"Head of the yearbook committee."

Small talk. From the look on his face, Franco disliked it as much as she did. Fortunately, they'd reached the director's office, so Aubrey rapped on the door.

Mrs. Kane smiled at her first sight of Aubrey... and her eyebrows disappeared behind her bangs when she spotted Franco standing beside her.

"I have a question," Aubrey said. "More like a request, really. Would you have a few minutes to come to my room, so that

Franco won't be in violation of any rules by coming in?"

"Now?"

"If you have the time, yes."

The woman thought about it for a moment, then looked at Franco. "I didn't realize you were on the schedule today."

"I'm not. Just stopped by to deliver this." He held up the package. "To Aub—To Ms. Brewer."

Aubrey couldn't imagine what it could be. Or why he'd brought it at all. Could her mother have been right? *Was Franco some sort of swindler who preyed upon helpless, wealthy dying women? In that case,* Bree, *you have nothing to fear, being poor as a church mouse and all.*

"I just finished two new paintings," she said, "and I'm dying—no pun intended, honest—to show them off. I can't get Franco's opinion from out in the hall. I can't carry them out so he can see them, and he can't come in to carry them for me. See my dilemma?"

"I wouldn't mind seeing your latest works myself," Kane said. "I'm no art critic, but I know what I like." She glanced at her watch, then stood and shouldered her purse strap. "But can it wait until tomorrow? I have a dinner date with my husband."

Mrs. Kane walked between Franco and Aubrey to the door, and linking arms with both, said, "Oh, don't look so glum, kids. It's an archaic rule, but without rules, we'd have anarchy, now wouldn't we?"

"I suppose," Aubrey said. She'd had a headache since getting up this morning, and now she felt woozy, as well. She knew her limits, and had come perilously close to exceeding them. The headaches and dizzy spells had always come without warning, but lately, they'd been worse and more frequent.

"I hate to be a party pooper, but I think maybe we should conclude this little gathering."

The director took one look at her and nodded. "Excellent idea. You're looking a mite peaked today."

Aubrey met Franco's eyes. "Please don't think I'm an ungrateful twit. I appreciate that you came all the way down here on your day off, just to deliver that." She pointed at the gift.

"Hey, it's okay. Really. Don't give it another thought." He held out the package.

"Okay, I'll take it, but I'll wait until next time I see you to open it."

One corner of his mouth lifted in a slow grin. He was quite handsome, in a rugged sort of way.

"Sure, no problem," he said. "You need help getting to your room?"

"No, the dizzy spell has passed. I'll be fine. But thanks."

He and Mrs. Kane walked her as far as the elevator, and left Aubrey to return to her room alone.

The last thing she expected to see was her mother in the easy chair, bare feet propped on the flowery ottoman and nonchalantly leafing through a magazine.

"There you are," she said. "I told myself 'give her five minutes, then call in the militia!'"

Aubrey sat on the footrest, hoping her mother hadn't noticed her hesitant, slightly unsteady steps.

"I think if the weather is decent tomorrow, we should get manicures and pedicures. Have lunch at The Gryphon. Maybe wander through the arboretum. I'll call and make reservations, and pick you up at ten in the morning."

Evidently, she'd gone home and given some thought to the way she'd talked to Franco. This invitation, Aubrey knew, was the closest she'd get to an apology from her mother.

"Lovely as that sounds," she began, "I don't have the stamina for an action-packed day like that. Maybe we could

just have lunch. It isn't like anyone but the undertaker is going to see my nails, anyway."

Agnes rolled her eyes, and Aubrey braced herself for another "why must you be so morose" lecture.

"You might have the energy if you'd stop wasting it on
your morbid sense of humor and that… that *janitor*."

Aubrey threw off her scarf and ran both hands through
what was left of her hair. "Please, Mama, not today, okay?"

Agnes exhaled a martyr-like sigh. "Have you had supper
yet?"

"There's a salad and a sandwich in the mini-fridge. I
might pick at them later."

"Bree…"

It was Aubrey's turn to sigh. The challenge of keeping a
civil tongue in her head when her mother behaved this way
was downright exhausting. The headaches were almost con-
stant now and her muscle strength seemed to wane by the
hour. She looked longingly at her walker, standing near the
windows on the other side of the room. She'd held off as long
as she could. Like it or not—and she did not—the time had
come to use it whenever she was on her feet. How much
longer, Aubrey wondered, before she'd have to trade it for a
wheelchair? Before her reasoning skills diminished and her
eyesight declined?

"Would you do me a favor, Mama, and bring my walker
over here? I'd like to wash up and get ready for bed while
you're still here with me."

Agnes was on her feet in a heartbeat. "I'm so glad you've
come to your senses. I was beginning to think I'd have to hire
a full-time nurse to watch your every move, since vanity
wouldn't allow you to use it before now." She put it down in
front of Aubrey with a metallic clunk. "At the pharmacy the
other day, I saw the most adorable little basket, made just
for walkers. Three sections. Nice and deep. Why, it even had
a cup holder! Tomorrow on my way here, I'll stop and get it,
and put it on for you."

"Does it have streamers?"

"Why no…"

"A little bell? Better still, one of those bulbous horns, like the trained seals use at the circus?"

"Oh, you," Agnes said with a wave of her hand. "Always teasing, just like your father."

Aubrey pulled herself up and leaned on the walker's handlebars. What had the physical therapist said? Lift then push, or the other way around? If she had the strength, she'd pick up the stupid contraption and slam it down, over and over again, until it looked as battered and bent as she felt. Oh, how she *hated* this tumor! It had already taken so much, and now, the slow erosion of her memory, her once-precise diction…

Agnes slid an arm around her, the other hand guiding the walker into the bathroom. "Push it, darlin', just a little," she said, "then take a step. Not too fast, though. There you go. Now another push… step… that's it. See there? You've got the hang of it. And the more you use it, the easier it'll be!"

The sweetness of her mother's guidance took her back to her sixth birthday, when Agnes had spent countless hours patiently teaching her to ride her two-wheeler, sans the reliable training wheels. The memory made Aubrey yearn for those years before Agnes's dreams superseded her own. Made her want to cry, too. The weighty bike promised exhilaration and fun… once she'd got the hang of it. But this thing? The contraption was quite literally moving her closer to the grave, step by painful step.

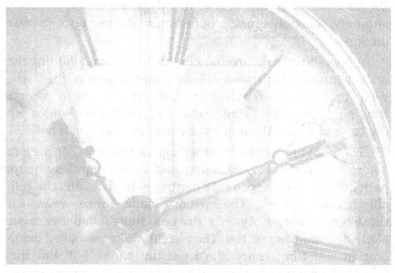

Chapter Fourteen

ONE LIGHT RAP AND AUBREY'S DOOR SLOWLY OPENED, emitting a low-pitched creak. *Few squirts of machine oil will fix that right up,* Franco told himself. A quick scan of the room told him that she was alone.

And then the breath caught in his throat at the sight of Aubrey, fast asleep in the big flowery chair, clutching an open book to her chest. Her head scarf had formed a silky blue and green puddle on the floor. Had it slipped off, or had she grown weary of repeatedly repositioning it and tightening the knot, and thrown it down there in a moment of frustration?

A slight furrow appeared in her brow as, shoulders hunched, she tried to cuddle deeper into the cushions. Jill had done the same thing on nights when, after tossing and turning, her blankets slid to the foot of the bed. A futile attempt at warmth, and it bothered him, seeing Aubrey's discomfort.

He spotted his gift on the coffee table. Spied a bright patchwork quilt, too, neatly folded over the back of her desk chair. Taking care not to wake her, Franco grabbed it. *If you get caught in here...* The instant he tucked it under her chin, her features relaxed. If he got caught, so be it. He searched his mind for a word to describe the feeling that burned in his chest. She exhaled a whispery sigh, and he knew: tenderness.

Franco walked to the door and quietly pulled it shut behind him. *Giving up the booze has turned you into a sappy old fart,* he thought, making his way to the elevator. A glance into the ornate mirror beside it took him by surprise. It had been a long, long time since he'd looked this calm, rested...

content. Hands pocketed, he smiled all the way down to the first floor, and kept right on smiling as stepped onto the porch.

"Trying to earn brownie points?"

He looked toward the craggy voice.

"Hey, Dusty. What're you still doing out here?"

"Waiting for you to make good on your promise." He glanced at a nonexistent watch. "Ten minutes, huh?"

Franco hadn't forgotten. But the trip to Kane's office, then checking in on Aubrey…

"Isn't it past your bedtime?"

It wasn't likely the kid would grin, even if he got the joke. Franco couldn't remember a single time when he'd seen the boy look anything but grim. Or angry. Well, there was that moment during their little set-to… since then, Dusty had been a whole lot more respectful, at least when Franco was around.

"You know I'm sixteen, right?"

He slid a rocker closer to the wheelchair. "I would have guessed seventeen."

"Whatever." Dusty snorted. "Where's that package you were carrying?"

"I delivered it."

"Yeah? Who's it for?"

"Aub—ah, Mrs. Brewer. It's an art book."

"Don't know if coming in on your day off will impress Mrs. Kane, but that's sure to help you score with Aubrey."

Franco winced. "Score? That's the last thing on my mind. But since you're up on pretty much everything around here, you probably already know that."

"Yeah, I guess."

"How often do you come out here after dark?"

"A lot. Nearly every day, but only when I'm sure every-body else is asleep."

"I liked being alone, too, when I was your age. But I'll bet you're not out here thinking about test scores or the idiot in PE class who thinks squirting shampoo in people's eyes is hilarious."

"Wait." Dusty leaned forward slightly. "Somebody did that to you?"

"*Once.*"

That produced a grin.

"How'd you figure out who it was?"

"I was pretty lucky in that regard... just one idiot to contend with."

"Did you get even?"

"Dunno that I'd call what I did *getting even,* exactly." Franco leaned back, stretched out his legs and crossed his ankles. "Well, I figured since the boob got such a kick out of pranking people," he said, linking fingers behind his head, "he'd enjoy *being* pranked, too." Dusty crossed his arms.

"First, I pulverized a bunch of those red tablets that come in Easter egg dye kits, and poured the dust into a sandwich bag. Then I sneaked into the locker room after school, unscrewed a shower head, and—"

"How'd you know which shower he'd use? There were, like, two dozen of 'em in my locker room."

"This guy thought he owned the place. And since he always claimed the shower head in the corner as his own..."

Dusty laughed. A genuine, knee-slapping, raucous laugh.

"No way, dude!"

Franco smirked. "Oh, believe me, yes way." Chuckling now himself, he reached over and gave Dusty's shoulder a playful slap. "But if you repeat any of this, I'll deny it."

"It's been, like, fifty years since you were in school," he teased. "The guy's probably dead... killed by somebody else he pranked." He went quiet for a moment, then added, "Man oh man. Did the guy, like, totally *freak*?"

"You could say that. For a minute there, I thought his voice box might explode."

Grinning like the Cheshire cat, Dusty shook his head. "Oh, man. That would've been awesomely cool to see." He paused, then added, "Did you get caught?"

"Nope. That bozo never figured out who was responsible for making him walk around all day looking like Captain Marvel."

Dusty snickered. "Bet he never pulled a stunt like that again, did he?"

"Not that I know of."

Something akin to admiration flickered on Dusty's wan face. *You're not the best role model, Allessi.* But then, it wasn't like Dusty would race to school and attempt the trick any time soon.

"So what kinda art book did you give her?" the boy asked, pointing at the package.

"It's a biography of sorts, about Bob Ross."

"That art guy Aubrey's always raving about?"

"One and the same."

"Bo-o-ring-g-g."

He gave the kid's arm another teasing whack. "Don't let her hear you say that."

"Yeah. She's a noob, all right."

"A *what*?"

"Gimme a minute here, to figure out how I'd explain it to my grandparents."

"Hey," Franco sat up, feigning shock. "They've got at least fifteen years on me."

"What is it you old folks love to say? 'If the shoe fits…?'" Dusty cackled. "So anyway, I guess you'd say a noob is somebody who's behind the times. A person who loves vintage stuff. Record players, reel-to-reel tape recorders, rotary phones…" He started counting on his fingers. "Somebody who's into oldies-but-goodies tunes, black-and-white movies and TV shows. You know, a person who's out of touch. But it isn't Aubrey's fault. She's, like, *forty* or something."

"You make it sound ancient." He leaned forward to get a better look at Dusty's face. "Is it my imagination, or are you shivering?"

The smile vanished like the flame of a snuffed candle.

"A little. But I don't want to go in yet."

Someone had left an afghan folded over the back of Franco's chair, and after retrieving his jacket, draped it over the boy's shoulders. "There," he said, "that oughta buy you another fifteen minutes or so."

Dusty looked up at Franco. "You're not leaving yet, are you?"

"If I had half a brain I would. I left dishes in the sink, and towels in the dryer that need folding. Didn't make my bed, either, to save time when I change the sheets tonight."

"Gee. Never figured you for the housewifey type." If disappointment could be graded, Dusty's expression would earn high marks.

"All that can wait," he said, checking his watch. "But only until the afghan doesn't fend off the night air anymore."

He leaned back again as Dusty said, "Why haven't you asked me why I'm here?"

"You just told me why."

"No, not why I'm out *here*," Dusty said. "Why I'm at Savannah Falls."

Franco shrugged. "It's none of my business."

"You're not curious?"

"I'd be lying if I said I wasn't. But I figure if you wanted to talk about it, you would."

"I have non-Hodgkin's Lymphoma. Stage Four. They gave me six cycles of garbage: Bleomycin. Vinblastine. Dacarbazine. And when none of that worked, they hit me with radiation. Cyclophosphamide. Vincristine." He hung his head, clenched his fists. "There's just one thing left to try. Brentux-imab vedotin. But my parents nixed it. Said it might cause a brain infection that, if it doesn't kill me, could permanently paralyze me."

"Jeez, you sound like a pharmacist."

"What else is there to do when you're *dying* except read up on what's killing you?"

Franco shook his head. A few clichés came to mind. Keep the faith. Don't lose hope. Miracles happen every day. But if he didn't believe any of that, how could he convince Dusty to buy it?

"Has Aubrey painted a portrait of you?" Franco asked instead.

"Sheesh. I hope not." He faked a laugh. "How corny would *that* be?"

"She painted one of me…"

The boy's eyebrows rose. "Yeah?"

"Yeah. And it's a real good likeness, too." He scrolled to the picture he'd snapped with his cell phone and handed it to Dusty.

"I was right," the boy said, grinning. "She's a noob. And so are you." But he was smiling when he handed the phone back. "Who's the woman in the other picture?"

"That's Jill." He pocketed the phone. "My wife."

"What happened to her?"

Franco tensed. How much of the truth could Dusty handle? How much did he want to tell?

"She died. Little more than three years ago. Car wreck."

"Is that how you got that scar on your chin?"

Most people didn't even notice, since it followed the line of his jaw. Instinct made him touch it.

"What else?"

He met the boy's eyes. "What else?"

"If the accident killed your wife, you didn't walk away with just that little cut on your face. So what else happened to you? I mean, were you a noob before the crash, too?"

"You're kind of a smart ass, aren't you?"

Dusty returned his grin. "So I've heard."

"I was in ICU for a week. Then rehab. Then physical therapy." It wasn't until they'd weaned him from the meds that he turned to whiskey to dull the pain. But Dusty didn't need to know he'd been a weak-kneed, self-pitying drunk. He rubbed his left wrist, worked the kinks out of his neck. "I can predict rain better than Matt Devitt on Channel 3."

"Same as my grandfather."

They shared a moment of silence before Franco got to his feet. "Well, this old man needs to drag his weary bones home." He laid a hand on Dusty's shoulder. "And you need to get into your room."

Then he turned the chair and pushed it through the entry doors, stopping a few feet shy of Aubrey, who stood in the lobby, leaning on a walker.

"How long have you been standing there?" Dusty asked.

She looked straight at Franco, a sweet smile on her face as she said, "Exactly long enough."

Chapter Fifteen

"I WAS GONNA SAY I CAN MAKE IT UPSTAIRS ON MY OWN," Dusty whispered. "But you might as well take me to my room." He looked up at Franco. "At least that way, you'll have a legitimate excuse for being on the third floor. Again."

"The tumor hasn't affected my hearing, you know."

"I thought you were napping," Franco said.

"I was. Then I noticed someone had stolen a very meticulously wrapped gift I received this afternoon, and thought I'd hunt down the thief."

"You found him." Had she noticed it, poking out of his inside jacket pocket? "But I wasn't stealing it. I have something at home I want to add to the package, is all."

"Franco. You didn't have to get the first present, let alone add another."

"*Bo-o-oring*," Dusty repeated, under his breath this time.

Thankfully, Aubrey chose to ignore the crack. "I'm surprised you're still here."

"Ran into this munchkin on my way out, see, and we've been talking."

"You and Mr. Mums-the-word? Talking?" She laughed. "You must have slipped him some sodium pentothal." She stepped aside to make room for Franco to roll Dusty's chair farther into the lobby.

"I changed my mind." He patted the package. "Soon as we tuck Dusty the Drifter in for the night, you can open that. I'll get the, uh, the other thing to you tomorrow. Or whenever."

They took their time getting to the elevators, and when Dusty pressed the up button, the afghan slipped from his shoulders. "Aw, rats," he said, "I forgot about this."

It had bunched up at the small of his back, and Aubrey couldn't help smiling a little as Franco gently tugged it free. "I'll put it where it goes on my way out," Franco said, flinging it over one shoulder.

And then they waited for the car to arrive, staring up and blinking with each *bing* that turned the floor numbers bright green.

These past few days, as Dusty slipped deeper into his own dark thoughts, Aubrey worried it meant he'd given up. When she heard him laughing out there on the porch, tears of joy had stung her eyes. No one had been able to reach Dusty. Not family or friends, not the staff, not even Dr. Robinson. Somehow, Franco had reached him, and it only underscored how wrong her mother had been.

Now, with Dusty secure in his room, Franco bent at the waist, putting himself eye level with the boy. "You want Grandpa to tuck you in?"

And there it was again, the big silly grin the boy had donned while Franco told his fake-blood shower story.

"Guess the nurses didn't tell you," he said. "I bite."

Franco's laughter filled the hall… and swelled Aubrey's heart.

"You don't scare me, Fido." He palmed the boy's cell phone, pecked his number into the contacts section, and handed it back. "Call me, any time, day or night, for any reason."

"How will you know it's me?"

"Because I added you to my contacts list, too. Don't look so surprised. Some noobs are tech-savvy." He winked and said, "Now go to bed."

They left him and walked toward Aubrey's room. "Noob?" she asked.

"People like you and me, who aren't hip and with it."

"Hmpf. I don't know about you, but I'm as hip and with it as they come."

He didn't look convinced, so she said, "Are you ready to break some rules?"

"I, ah…"

Judging by the dubious look on his face, Franco had second thoughts, maybe even thirds. But he followed her inside, and waited until she dropped into the big easy chair to move her walker aside.

"There are sodas in the mini-fridge," she said. "How about grabbing us a couple?"

"Choose your poison," he said, peering inside, "root beer or ginger ale?"

"Oh, ginger ale, for sure." Her stomach had been acting up for days. Soda crackers and ginger ale were the only things that didn't come right back up.

He opened the can for her. "Ice and a tumbler?"

"No, this is fine." Then, grinning, Aubrey said, "Tumbler? You really *are* a noob, aren't you?" He sat in the chair across from hers. "So what's the occasion?" she asked, and pointed to his gift.

Franco picked it up and handed it to her. "Just a little something to thank you for the painting. I hung it beside a picture of my wife. The way they're positioned, it's almost as though we're looking at each other."

"I'm glad you like it." Aubrey slid the envelope from under the satiny ribbon. She'd heard him tell Dusty how he lost his wife. And she'd been spot-on with her guess that he'd been with her when she died, too. He'd glossed over his recovery, though, and she had a feeling there was a whole lot more to the story than that.

The card he'd chosen—a tranquil lake surrounded by a forest ablaze with autumn color—roused a tiny gasp. How could he have known, when she'd never told anyone about the dream that she hoped would be her final wish? Hands trembling, she opened it and read the simple inscription:

Thank you hardly seems enough, so I hope you'll enjoy this.

Franco

Aubrey stood the card on the end table. "Since it's a sure bet I won't celebrate my next birthday, I'm going to pretend it's a birthday card, and leave it right here so I can enjoy it for a while." She picked up the package. "Where did you find paper just like mine?"

"Wrapped around your painting. I mean my painting."

Not a rip or a wrinkle, she noticed. "Just look at those precise corners, and the perfectly folded ends."

"If you're gonna do a thing, might as well do it right," he said.

"This is beyond right. It tells me you're a tad OCD. I am, too, so that's a good thing."

A very good thing. She'd been thinking about asking him to do her a favor, the biggest she'd ever asked of anyone. He'd need every ounce of courage he could muster… if she could convince him to say yes.

"I like you, Franco Allessi. You're a very good man."

His brow furrowed slightly in response to her odd, ill-timed compliment. *No matter,* Aubrey thought. She'd answer all of his unasked questions… just as soon as she asked one of her own.

Under the wrapper, Aubrey found a book, and read the title aloud: *Happy Trees, Happy Clouds.* Aubrey opened her mouth to thank him for the thoughtful gift, but a sob choked off her voice. She met his eyes. "I… I love it." Hugging it to her chest, Aubrey said, "Thank you. Thank you so much."

He shrugged and bobbed his head, looking self-conscious and out of place. Because he feared Mrs. Kane would find out he'd violated the 'do not enter' rule? Or because his gift had touched her to the point of tears?

The latter, she decided; his interaction with Dusty was all the proof she needed.

"Nice painting," he said with a glance toward her most recent work.

He'd singled out the canvas she'd offhandedly titled "The Harvest." It was her turn to shrug.

"What, you don't like it?"

"Don't look so surprised. I can count on one hand the number of my own paintings that I'm truly happy with." She looked at the one leaning on the easel's legs. "And that isn't one of them."

"Looks good to me. Real good."

"I watched one of my Bob Ross DVDs yesterday. Watched it three times, as a matter of fact. But I couldn't come close to duplicating what he produced in the video. And to think he created every painting in a thirty-minute segment for TV."

"You don't think they filmed for hours, and edited it down to fit the programming?"

"I hope not. I want to believe he was just that talented." Aubrey got to her feet. Could she make it as far as the easel without the aid of her walker? It only took one step to realize that she could not.

Franco anticipated her need and went to her.

"There's no shame in leaning on others once in a while, y'know."

He offered his arm. For a moment, she considered sitting back down. Instead, she took it, let him guide her to the canvas.

"I'm one of those people who can't draw a stick person, so if you're about to explain why this isn't beautiful, you'll have to talk as if I'm in preschool."

He didn't realize it, but Franco had played right into her plans. Aubrey had never considered herself the manipulative sort, but she simply had to make her dream come true before she died.

"I tried Ross's fan brush technique," she began, "and then I realized… it isn't the tools. It isn't the lighting. I can't dupli-cate the colors because I've never seen autumn leaves in person."

"Seriously?"

She shook her head. "I've lived here all my life, and ex-cept for annual summer vacations to my grandparents' cabin in Pennsylvania, I've never left Georgia." She hesitated. "You look surprised."

"A little, yeah. I figured with your art background, you might have done a semester or two in Paris or Madrid. Fig-ured you had the stamps of foreign cities on every page of your passport."

"I might have, if not for my mother." She waved away the unpleasant thought. "So how long have you been in Savan-nah?"

"Just a couple years."

His face took on a far-off, forlorn expression, and she wondered what memory of his wife had inspired it.

"Now that you mention it," he said, "the fall colors here aren't nearly as…"

"Vivid?"

"Yeah. Vivid. They don't hold a candle to what happens to the trees up north."

Eyes narrowed slightly, he tilted his head and studied her face. "You're looking a little green around the gills. What-say we get you back to your chair. Then I'm gonna leave, so you can get some—"

"No! You can't leave yet," she said, mustering all her strength to grip his arm. "I… I need to ask you something."

He guided her to the cushions, and then moved her soda closer. "Okay," he said, returning to the chair, "shoot."

"How comfortable are you in this place?"

"Not very." He chuckled. "If *Krissi* finds out I'm in here…" He drew a forefinger across his throat.

"No, not here in my room, silly. I mean here at Savannah Falls. Does it bother you, being surrounded by death?"

He flinched. "Jeez. You don't beat around the bush, do you?"

"It's a waste of time, and unnecessarily hard on the shrubbery. Being a plant guy, you should appreciate that analogy. Besides, I don't have the luxury of wasting time." Aubrey took a sip of the ginger ale. "Look," she began, "I need to know exactly how comfortable you are, being close to someone who's about to meet her maker... being around her for an extended period of time."

"I'm not following you."

"Well, see, it's like this. I've been doing a little research. A ton of research, actually. Did you know there are places right here in Georgia that have autumn leaves? *Real* autumn leaves that positively glow? Cadmium yellow. Alizarin crimson. Juane orange..." She hid behind her hands, just long enough to get hold of herself. "Listen to me, rambling on and on. If I'm not careful, I'll put you to sleep. What would *Krissi* say about that!"

Franco only smiled. But she could see that he was still confused.

"There's a place up north, in the Blue Ridge Mountains. Lake Burton in Moccasin Creek State Park. In Clarksville." She pointed at her desk. "There's a file, right beside my laptop. See for yourself."

He leaned left, grabbed the folder, and began leafing through it as she continued.

"I need to check out campers. Or better still, RVs. You know, those ginormous things that entertainers travel in? The park has fully equipped campsites—water, electricity, the whole nine yards."

"Looks real nice," he said, closing the file. When he put it back on her desk, Franco picked up a framed photograph. "I saw this the other day, when that lunatic went nuts and knocked over your shelf unit. Who are these kids?"

"That reminds me, I haven't thanked you yet for putting everything back together so quickly, and all by yourself. You're a very *nice* man, too."

"I was happy to help. Couldn't have you thinking all men are bullies and brutes."

Aubrey returned his smile. "I was married just long enough to believe you."

Franco leaned forward, rested his elbows on his knees. "How did you lose him?"

"Cancer."

He winced. "Sorry for your loss."

Aubrey laughed. "*My* cancer," she said, "not his. Michael isn't a bad guy, really, but he's weak and self-centered. Chemo was tougher on him than me. Not because it hurt him to watch me suffer, mind you, but because once I started treatments, I didn't have the energy or time to focus all my attention on him. Oh, he gave it the old college try those first few months, but when people stopped telling him how great he was, there wasn't much in it for him. That, and the longer I was doing chemo, the worse things got.

"Michael fancies himself a writer, so when he left, he delivered a long poetic discourse, about how he was doing us both a favor by letting me concentrate solely on my health." Laughing again, she summed up with, "I imagine by now he found a way to write the fussy little speech into one of his vanity press-published novels."

"Oh, *he* sounds like a winner," Franco said, shaking his head. "It's none of my business, but I'd say you're better off without him."

Aubrey might have agreed, but that would only make her want to explain how her mother had set the Aubrey-Michael relationship in motion… and hadn't stopped nagging until she could introduce him as her son-in-law.

"Those kids in the picture, by the way," she said, changing the subject, "are my students. I teach art history at a small private high school. Correction: I *taught* at the Savannah School of the Arts."

He focused on the picture. "Looks like they think a lot of you."

"And the feeling is mutual." She sighed. "I sure do miss them."

He returned the picture to her desk. "Well, it's getting late. Anything I can do for you before I leave?"

"No," Aubrey said, "I'll be fine." She glanced at the book. "Thanks for the present. I'm going to climb into bed and read until I fall asleep." Tomorrow, she'd ask her mother to take her to the lake in Clarksville. It had been a crazy idea, anyway, thinking she could ask such a huge favor of a near stranger.

Chapter Sixteen

GETTING TO AND FROM SAVANNAH FALLS REQUIRED Franco to pass Bad Decisions, a small dive bar that catered to longshoremen and construction workers. The spinning neon sign—a guy with an angel on one shoulder and a devil on the other—seemed like a personal invitation. He could almost feel the sensation of cool Southern Select foam on his upper lip, and even from the road, he heard the steady *thump-thump* of the jukebox. It reminded him of all the nights he'd spent searching out songs about broken hearts and regret. He hoped the bar would never change its name—at least not while he had to walk past it twice a day—because it was a perfect reminder of what a bad decision it would be to set foot inside.

Today, he distracted himself with thoughts of the surprise he'd planned for Aubrey. He'd already run the idea past the principal and guidance counselor at the high school; all he needed now was a thumbs-up from Mrs. Kane.

The administrator wasn't in her office, and neither was her secretary. So he borrowed a Post-It from the assistant's desk and scribbled NEED TO RUN SOMETHING BY YOU, ASAP. WILL BE IN GAZEBO. He signed it FRANCO, added his cell number, and stuck it to her door.

While mowing around the structure a few days ago, Franco had noticed holes in the screens, probably put there by wheelchair footrests. Jill had taught him how to make temporary patches, and when a hunt for supplies in the tool shed proved fruitless, he decided to bring the stuff from home and make the repairs: a needle threaded with clear monofilament fishing line, a few squares cut from the roll of screening he'd stowed in his shed, and a few well-placed stitches would do until the center could work proper repairs into the budget. With that chore complete, he got onto his hands and knees to hammer popped-up nailheads back into the entrance ramp's boards.

"Now why do I get the idea that neither Amos nor Carl suggested this task?"

He looked up, shading his eyes from the bright sunshine.

"Morning, Mrs. Kane." He got to his feet, dusting pollen from the knees of his jeans. "I see you got my note."

"I did, indeed." She pointed over his shoulder. "Did you make those patches all on your own, too?"

"Well, Amos went to the garden center for mulch and border plants. Didn't see much point in standing around with my thumbs in my pockets until he got back."

"You could have gone home."

And miss an opportunity to shave another hour from his sentence? No way.

"A lot of the residents walk around in bedroom slippers," he explained, pointing at the few still-protruding nails. "Didn't want any of them getting snagged on these things."

Mrs. Kane smiled, and Franco decided she'd probably been a real knockout in her younger years.

"So what's this plan you want to run by me?"

"Last time I talked with Au—Mrs. Brewer, she said something about not living long enough to celebrate another birthday. And she misses her students. So I got this idea about getting them all over here. Her principal and guidance counselor liked the idea so well they offered to put the kids on a bus, arrange for cake, ice cream, streamers, balloons... all they need from us is a party room."

"Like the solarium?"

"That's what I was thinking. Plenty of tables and chairs, good lighting for photographs."

"I'll check the schedule," she said, "and find a date when it isn't booked for another activity. Would you like me to call the school? Make sure they know we're on board?"

"That'd be great." He scrolled through his cell phone's contacts, and as she wrote down the principal's number, he added, "Just one problem that I can think of."

"Oh?"

"Figuring out how to get her up there once the kids have things set up." And more important than that, coming up with a scheme to keep her crabby mother away from the celebration.

She patted his shoulder. "You leave that little detail to me. I'll make sure there's enough of everything so that we can invite everyone who's ambulatory. We haven't had an official get-together since Christmas, so the staff will love it."

The blue jay soared above them, smooth and slow, fingerlike wingtips flicking as it landed on the gazebo's cupola.

"He's quite a chatterbox, isn't he?"

Franco agreed. "And a stalker." He chuckled. "Not sure why, but the loudmouth makes a point of dive-bombing my head at least once a day."

"There are a lot of jays around here…"

"But only one with a split crest." He pointed at it. "Keep it up, Gilbert, and some hungry hawk will get you."

"Gilbert?"

"The comedian with the loud, grating voice?"

"Oh, him." Mrs. Kane laughed. "Well, I'll let you get back to work. Stop by the office on your way out, and I'll let you know what the principal said."

Franco flinched as the jay flew within inches of his head before landing in the branches of a nearby coral vine.

"I believe there are hard hats in the shed…"

"Thanks," he told her. Franco smirked. "What's the matter? Afraid the media will show up to investigate workplace violence on the grounds of the formerly serene Savannah Falls?"

Laughing, Mrs. Kane waved and headed back to the main building.

On his knees again, Franco returned to his hammering as the bird squawked.

"If you don't like the noise," he grumbled, "go visit your girlfriend until I'm done." He peeked at his watch. "I'm guessing she's in her room."

It flit away, and he knew where he'd find it if he had a mind to: in the tree outside Aubrey's window, head bobbing and squawking for all it was worth. He pictured her, too, smiling in her soft, sweet way as she mimicked its actions.

Would she enjoy the big surprise? Not if she was anything like Jill. His wife had hated being the center of attention, and he wouldn't have thrown her a second party on a bet. The thought roused the pleasant memory of the first—and only—shindig he'd organized for her. Just a small family get-together to celebrate her thirtieth birthday. Oh, she'd been gracious enough... until everyone left. Dark eyes flashing, she'd stood nose-to-nose with him and said, "If you ever, *ever* do anything like that again..." She'd nearly bowled him over, wrapping arms and legs around him to add, "I love you to pieces, you big lummox. So please don't make me do something we'll both regret," and punctuated the threat with a kiss that, even now, had the power to make his lips tingle.

It took three tries to hammer the last nail flush with the wood, because tears blurred his vision.

As he walked from the gazebo to the tool shed, his cell phone rang. Resting his backside against the stone wall beside it, he read the caller ID screen.

"What's up, boss?"

"Just wondering how many hours you have left over there."

"Why? Won't get my license back for months yet."

"Yeah, well, lemme put it this way: Ted gets lost every time he drives outta the parking lot. I'm thinking maybe if you went with him, you could, you know, navigate."

Franco had worked at the auto body shop for years, and this was the closest to a compliment Clayton had ever paid him. The guy must really be desperate to put a kid with so little experience behind the wheel of the tow truck.

"Who's Ted's backup?"

"Me."

Clayton liked sitting in his office, taking calls and barking orders. Dealing with the public wasn't his strong suit.

"I never should have agreed to let you work off all your hours at once." He exhaled a grating sigh. "When are you coming back?"

"Still have about twelve hours to go."

"Sheesh. You *are* coming back when you're finished, aren't you?"

Franco laughed quietly. "Maybe this would be a good time to ask for a raise."

"And maybe I need a guy in the cab who can operate the winch and the boom without forgetting to block the tires."

He'd heard that tone of voice more times than he cared to remember, and pitied the kid who'd been hearing it in his stead. "Easy, Clay. Wouldn't want that vein on your forehead to explode over something as minor as an out-of-alignment chock."

Clayton snorted. "If only things were that simple." A phone rang in the background. "Look, I need to get back to work. You comin' back when your time at the hospice is up or not?"

He pictured the steadily growing stack of bills on his kitchen counter and the quickly shrinking total in his checking account. It wasn't as though he had a lot of choices. "Sure, Clay, sure," he said. "Soon as I wrap things up here, I'll give you a heads up so you can put me on the schedule."

"I'm sure if Ted was here, he'd say thank you, too," Clayton said, and hung up.

Franco dropped the phone into his pocket and glanced up the hill, at the antebellum mansion-turned-hospice center that had changed...

... everything.

Chapter Seventeen

AS THE BUS ROLLED UP, FRANCO GOT HIS FIRST LOOK AT Aubrey's students.

Their fresh, expectant faces made him glad he'd looked her up in the school yearbook. In both pictures—the black-and-white headshot on the faculty page and the full-color shot of her as the girls' lacrosse coach—her vibrancy radiated from the pages. That's how the kids remembered her, and he owed it to them to issue a warning of sorts, as much for her sake as theirs.

When the doors hissed open, he stepped onto the bus, surprising the driver and everyone on board.

"Hey, guys," he said, ignoring the tremor in his voice, "my name's Franco, and I'd like to thank all of you for coming. Aubrey has no idea what's going on, and as you can probably guess, this is going to make her day." He chuckled. "Who am I kidding? This will make her *year*." If she lived that long...

He pointed toward the solarium roof, visible from the right side bus windows. "That's one of her favorite places here at the hospice. She's already up there, decorating the place for what she thinks is someone else's party."

The woman seated behind the driver rose and held out her hand. "Hello, Franco. I'm Muriel Peterson," she said, "school principal and a friend of Aubrey's. I can't tell you how much we appreciate what you're doing for her."

"Hey, I just came up with the idea. You guys are doing everything else."

The girl seated behind Mrs. Peterson said, "So it'll really be a surprise?"

"Totally," Franco said as the rest of the kids got to their feet. "But before we head inside, I thought I should give you a heads up. Mrs. Brewer isn't, ah, she might not look exactly the way you remember her."

"My grandmother died of cancer last year," said a kid in the back. "Those last couple months were brutal. She lost something like fifty pounds and all her hair."

"Yeah," another boy agreed. "Most of us know somebody with cancer, so don't worry. We won't stare, or say something stupid."

Nods and whispers of agreement floated throughout the small space, and Franco admitted to himself that if he'd been half as decent at their age, his life—and the lives of those closest to him—might have been a whole lot easier.

"That's a relief," he teased, drawing a hand across his forehead. "I was worried you'd take one look at her and run back to the bus, blubbering like babies."

Mrs. Peterson joined in the kids' laughter. "We've been looking forward to this all week. Every one of us loves Aubrey, and we've missed her, too." She gestured toward the folders, cardboard tubes, and colorful greeting-card envelopes each student held. "They've each made something for her, based on lessons she taught them."

"That's great," he said. "Way better than store-bought cards."

He led the way up the porch steps and into the lobby, where Mrs. Kane greeted them.

"It's such a pleasure to meet you," she said, grasping the principal's hand. And facing Franco, she added, "I'll have the cake brought upstairs while you show them the way."

Show them the way? *Him?* The guy who'd spent more time in a boozy fog lately than sober? There were so many things wrong with her comment that Franco didn't know where to begin.

"Let's take the stairs to the second floor," he said, "so that we'll all get up there at the same time."

He felt a little like the Pied Piper, sans the flute and pointy hat. The stairwell emptied into the far end of the hall, and as they stepped through the fire door, he said, "She'll be right around this corner at the end of the hall. I'll go down ahead of you and make sure she's distracted so she won't notice when you walk in."

"Should we yell 'surprise!'?" one girl asked.

He thought of all the half-dozing patients likely to be in the solarium at this time of day. "Is there a way to yell quietly?"

Laughing, Mrs. Peterson said they'd do their best to make a gentle entrance.

"Give me five minutes," he said, walking backwards, then turned and jogged toward the solarium.

Even before reaching the big double-entry doors, he spotted Mrs. Kane rolling a cart across the back of the room. Aubrey saw her, too, and helped her lift the white-boxed sheet cake from the cart to the table against the wall. When Aubrey made a move to lift the lid, Mrs. Kane stopped her.

"Let's keep it covered for now," she said, "to protect the icing from dust or pollen."

"Or bees and flies," Jake said. He aimed a bony finger at the glass louvers, high in the solarium's domed ceiling. "If you're gonna leave 'em open, least you could do is pop for screens. Some people are allergic to stings, y'know."

Laughing, Mrs. Kane squeezed Jake's shoulder. "Funny, but I don't remember seeing such a notation in your file."

Grinning up at her, Jake rolled his eyes. "Not me, woman. But I'm not the only who comes down here to enjoy the breeze."

Franco stepped up beside Aubrey. "Need any help arranging paper plates and plastic forks?"

Her back was to the door as she inspected the table. "No, I think we've got things covered. But thanks."

"If Aubrey needs your help, she will *ask* for it."

Franco instantly recognized the smooth, southern-accented voice. Had Mrs. Kane invited her? Or had some witch-like sixth sense lured her here today? *Great,* he thought. *Just great.* Hopefully, Aubrey's stuck-up mother could keep a lid on her sarcasm long enough for the kids to make an entrance. Because if she spoiled this for them or Aubrey...

"Good to see you, ma'am," he lied.

She unpursed her red-lipsticked mouth, no doubt to hit him with another slur. Lucky for Franco, the kids chose that moment to burst into the room.

"Mrs. Brewer!" they said together. "Surprise!"

Aubrey whirled around and hid a tiny gasp of pleasure behind both hands as they surrounded her.

Franco stepped up to Mrs. Kane and the principal, watching Aubrey exchange hugs and cheek-kisses with the kids, chatting and laughing as tears of pure pleasure glittered in her blue eyes.

The director exhaled a wistful sigh. "How could I ever have thought this was a bad idea?"

Franco shot her a sideways glance. "You did?"

She waved away his disbelief. "Yes, but only for a moment." She winked. "Or two."

"Because you thought this might be too much for her, no doubt," the principal said.

"Yes, and a little much for the kids too."

Mrs. Peterson said, "But thanks to Franco, they were properly prepared." She beamed. "Look at them. Just *look* at them!"

It felt good, watching Aubrey interact with students she hadn't seen in months... some from this year's class, others from past semesters.

He tensed when Agnes joined them. "I can't believe my eyes," she said. "Why, she's positively glowing." Reaching around the principal and Franco, she squeezed Mrs. Kane's forearm. "Thank you. Thank you so much. I haven't seen her this happy since… since before the diagnosis."

The director patted Agnes's hand. "Don't thank me, dear. This was entirely Franco's doing." Facing the principal, she added, "Would you like to help me poke some candles into that cake?"

The women left him alone with Agnes, and as Franco tried to think of a logical reason to escape her, she said, "*You did all this?*"

"Well, I came up with the original idea…" He braced himself for a good old-fashioned southern gentlewoman scolding.

"But… *why?*"

Should he tell her the truth, or make something up and hotfoot it out of there? Franco thought of a great line from an old Jack Nicholson movie: "You can't handle the truth."

"I'll tell you why I did it. I did it because my greatest regret since my wife's death is that I never got to say goodbye." He ignored her surprised expression and glanced at Aubrey. "I figured I could spare her feeling that way, at least about those kids." He gave a quick, one-shouldered shrug. "She deserves this. *That's* why I did it."

Agnes' cheeks flushed as she pressed a palm to her chest. *She wouldn't be a half-bad-looking woman,* Franco thought, *if she smiled more often.*

"I… I don't know what to say, Mr. Allessi."

"There's nothing *to* say, except 'Happy early birthday, Aubrey.' Or 'Happy late birthday.' And please. Call me Franco."

He walked up to the cake table, helped himself to two squares—one for Amos, one for himself—and left the solarium. There'd be time, later, to see how Aubrey enjoyed the party.

He hoped.

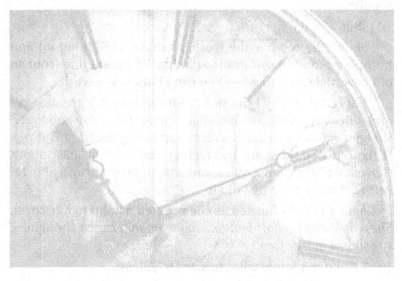

Chapter Eighteen

AUBREY COULDN'T RECALL THE LAST TIME SHE'D enjoyed a full, uninterrupted night's sleep. But last night, she had slept, and dreamed...

... of herself in front of the classroom, discussing Henri Gerves's style, explaining and demonstrating his methods, walking between the rows of art tables to help the kids import the techniques into their assignment.

She dreamed of the cabin her grandparents rented every summer in Pennsylvania's Allegheny Mountains.

Her dad's red kayak, slicing through the Apalachicola River near Georgia's Blood Mountain.

The image conjured a memory of their one—and only—fishing trip. They'd stood hip-deep in the warm water as a canopy of bright green sheltered them from the glaring sun. "Bet it's pretty here in the fall," she'd told him. His slow, southern drawl had taken on a reflective tone when he replied, "Only thing prettier is you, cupcake."

Tossing the covers aside, Aubrey stretched and yawned, unaware of the width of her smile... until she caught a glimpse of herself in the mirror above her dresser. Franco was responsible for this upbeat mood, she knew. Just yesterday, she'd considered emptying every Levetiracetam tablet in the amber-colored vial into her palm and washing them down with fizzing ginger ale. If the prescribed dose could diminish twitching, tremors, and mini-convulsions—and make her drowsy—surely an overdose would slow her breathing to the point of *not* breathing. Thoughts of Agnes, reacting to the news that her only child had taken her own life, stopped her.

After a quick shower, Aubrey dressed and had breakfast, then gathered her paint kit and headed for the gazebo. Passing the walker on her way out, she considered using it. But the kit wouldn't fit in the basket, and she felt strong enough to make the short walk without it.

A commotion outside Dusty's room stopped her.

"What's going on?" she whispered to a nurse.

"Poor kid's in bad shape today, real bad," the woman said, shaking her head. "We had to call the family, in case…" She let silence complete the sentence for her.

Heart hammering with dread, Aubrey stepped into Dusty's dimly lit, hushed room and dropped her paint kit on the dresser beside potted plants and greeting cards. His mother reached out, grasped her hand. "Oh, Aubrey, I'm so glad you're here. Dusty listens to you. Say something, will you please?"

Say something? Like what? she wondered. It would be hypocritical, given what she'd almost done yesterday, to say, "You still have a lot to live for!" or "Open your eyes, kiddo, you're scaring people" or "Don't be a wuss. Sit up and fight!"

Dusty's older brother got up, gestured toward the chair beside the bed, and Aubrey dropped into it. She noticed the untouched breakfast tray on Dusty's hospital bed table and, fighting tears, said, "Don't tell me you're going to let your breakfast go to waste, *again*." She lifted the aluminum cover, let it clatter onto the tabletop. "Oh, wow. Your favorite… French toast." She rummaged through the silverware, hoping the sound of metal against metal might rouse him. "Mind if I help myself? Oh, of course you don't. I'll just have a bite. Or three."

The only sounds in the room were the soft murmurs of family members, and his mother's quiet tears, as they watched and waited…

"Funny," Aubrey said, her voice cracking slightly, "but I never figured you for a lazy kid. Sarcastic? Yes. Impertinent? You bet. But lazy? No way."

She watched his face and held her breath when his eyeballs moved left and right beneath closed lids. His family noticed it, too, and stepped up closer to his bed.

"Gonna get fat," he mumbled, "eating all those carbs."

Such relief flooded through her that she gasped and slumped forward, forehead resting on his arm. But she needed to get hold of herself, for the sake of all those gathered here. She swallowed. Hard. Then said, "You don't want to know what happened to the last guy who called me fat."

He opened one eye to say, "You ate him?"

Nervous laughter filled the space, because despite this glimmer of hope, Dusty wasn't out of the woods just yet.

On her feet now, Aubrey realized she needed to finish his painting, and soon.

"Thank you," his mom said, hugging her again. "I just knew you could get through to him."

"Don't give her so much credit," the kid grated out. "I only opened my eyes 'cause I figured we could get rid of her sooner."

When Aubrey saw the left corner of his mouth lift, she gave his big toe a gentle pinch. "Better watch it," she teased. "Smiling will destroy your mean and nasty reputation."

Before cancer invaded his body, he'd been a big, burly kid. Now he looked small and weary, and nearly as white as the pillowcase. If it hurt her this much, how much more devastated were his loved ones? She said her goodbyes to his parents and siblings, gathered up her art kit, and left them to enjoy their time with Dusty. A few steps into the hall, she leaned against the wall, gathering her wits. When she'd moved into Savannah Falls, Dusty had already been a resident for more than a month. Considering her oncologist's prognosis, it had seemed reasonable to expect that she'd die first. Seeing him so still and quiet frightened her, not only because she'd miss him when he was gone, but because it underscored her own mortality. If she was going to make her dream come true, she couldn't put it off any longer.

And to think you nearly took matters into your own hands yesterday, she thought.

Moving was a struggle, and Aubrey wished she'd used her walker. Wished she'd remembered to bring Dusty's painting, too. She glanced down the hall. Ten or twelve steps, that's all it would take to get to her room and collect both. Could she make it without assistance? *If you want to finish that watercolor, you* have *to make it.*

Slowly, she moved along the wall, one hand following the chair rail to steady herself. It took fifteen minutes to travel the short distance, and once there, Aubrey was exhausted and out of breath. It scared her, realizing how quickly her strength was waning. The trip to the mountains couldn't wait.

She dialed her mother's number, and when Agnes answered, said, "Are you planning to stop by any time soon?"

"Not today, dear. I have garden club this morning, and it's my afternoon to mind the hospital gift shop."

"Oh. Right. Of course." *How silly of me to think you'd rearrange your life for your almost-dead only child!*

Aubrey immediately regretted her self-centered thought. She wanted her mother to live as normal a life as possible now, so that getting on with her life would be easier after the funeral.

"What do you need, Bree?"

"I have a question to ask you, and I'd rather not do it over the phone."

"I'll come by tonight, on my way home from the hospital."

"You won't be too tired?"

Agnes chuckled. "Not as tired as you. Get some rest, now, and I'll see you in a few hours."

Aubrey didn't feel like hiking all the way to the gazebo, not even while leaning on her walker. If she asked, an orderly would gladly take her there by way of a wheelchair, but the mood had passed. Stretching out on the bed, she decided to take a short nap. Later she'd make her way back down to Dusty's room to see how he was doing. Maybe by then she'd feel more like painting.

"Can I get you anything, Mrs. Brewer?"

Groggy, headachy, and slightly dizzy, she levered herself onto one elbow and recognized Lauren, the day nurse. Aubrey glanced at the tableside clock. How could she have slept for nearly three hours!

"Could you give me a hand getting to my walker?"

The smiling nurse obliged, then doled out Aubrey's afternoon medications. "Be sure to drink *all* of this water, now," she advised. "We don't want you getting dehydrated."

Aubrey had never liked needles, and since the diagnosis, she'd grown to hate them. The very thought of a rehydrating IV made her shiver involuntarily. "No, we certainly don't want that."

The nurse helped her to her feet. "I'll be back shortly to check on you."

As she made her way to the door, Aubrey asked about Dusty's condition.

"His family is downright jubilant, despite the fact that he's complaining."

"Complaining about what?"

"That we didn't let him, you know, go." Hospital speak, she knew, for *die.*

"Do you think he's up to a little company?"

"Physically? Sure. But he's still Dusty, so don't go in there expecting a civil conversation."

"Thanks," she said, hoping the woman would go about her business, because if the trip back to Dusty's room was as difficult as the trip here, she'd insist on putting Aubrey into a wheelchair. And she wasn't ready for that just yet.

When finally she reached his door, Aubrey saw Dusty sitting in his usual place—wheelchair facing the windows—

staring out at the rolling green lawn. Was he imagining himself out there, kicking a soccer ball, playing catch with one of his brothers, tossing a Frisbee to his dog? He'd been quite the athlete before...

Aubrey sighed. "Hey, kiddo. It's me."

"Duh," he said. "I've only been listening to the *clunk-scrape* of your walker for the past fifteen minutes." He turned slightly to look her in the eye. "When are you gonna face facts and get yourself one of these?" He slapped the arm of his chair. "It would spare the rest of us having to listen to you, huffing and puffing like the big bad wolf."

"Good *God,* you can be mean," she said, frowning. "You aren't the only one around here who wishes things were different, you know."

Dusty raised one eyebrow.

"Oh, don't look so surprised. The staff *has* to coddle you. And your family? Well, they love you too much to tell you what you deserve to hear. But I'm not a nurse, and I'm not a relative. *I* get to be honest."

She parked herself in the straight-backed chair beside him. "You should have seen your folks this morning. Broke my heart to watch them, watching you. Don't you love them at *all* anymore?"

"What's love got to do with it?"

"Y'know, that was never one of my favorite songs."

He looked at her as if she'd grown a second nose, so she sang a few bars. When he winced, Aubrey laughed. "I think I've just figured out how to punish you for your surly attitude. I'll sing. Opera next time. Loudly."

Dusty held his palm parallel to the floor and wiggled the fingertips. "Ooh, I'm so scared. Although I'd hardly call that singing."

My, but he could be an insufferable brat! "You know what I think?"

He groaned. "No, but I'll bet you're gonna tell me."
She continued as if he hadn't spoken.

"I think you hate being spoiled and mollycoddled and treated like a little boy. I think your nasty disposition and smart-talk is your way of saying 'Back off, people, I'm sick, not stupid!' I think you're tired of avoiding reality and pretending this is an ordinary hospital, and that someday you'll get better and go home, and pick up right where you left off before they signed you into this room."

Dusty mulled that over for a second, then hung his head. "Whatever," he said, his voice a dull monotone.

Aubrey grabbed his hand, holding on despite his feeble attempt to free himself. "I'm scared too, kiddo. Terrified, if you want the truth. And I'm mad, too. Mad as hell. I want to know 'why me?' If I had the energy, I'd kick a wall or punch a door."

"What good would that do."

A statement, she noticed, not a question. Aubrey squeezed his hand. "Exactly," she said. "What good would it do."

She turned him loose, glanced around the room. "Hey, what happened to the Dusty-sized teddy bear that used to sit on your desk chair?"

Something akin to a chuckle popped from his throat. "I killed it."

It was Aubrey's turn to raise her eyebrows. "Now *that*," she said, "I would have paid to see."

Another ho-hum "Whatever," and then, "So were you really surprised at the party, or was that just a big act?"

"No, it was genuine. I was truly stunned." She couldn't help but smile, remembering the way the kids exploded into the room, then surrounded her. "I haven't had that much fun since before my oncologist said..." She lowered her voice to mimic the doctor's. "'Much as it pains me to say it, Mrs. Brewer, there's simply nothing more we can do for you. I strongly urge you to get your affairs in order.'"

"Yeah. What a load of crap. Like it really pains them." Dusty shook his head again. "Rich liars, that's all they are."

She could point out the unfairness of his statement, because most doctors cared a *lot.* But, as he'd so astutely pointed out earlier, what good would that do?

"So tell me, Dusty, what was your role in that little party scheme?"

"I was the lookout. Franco told me to sit by my window and watch for the bus to turn into the drive, then call his cell phone so he could meet your students in the lobby."

"Meet them? But why?"

"I, ah, I'm not sure."

The guilty gleam in his eyes proved the exact opposite. But *why* would Franco want to meet the kids before—

In an instant, she knew: he'd wanted to warn them about how much she'd changed. Only a good and decent man would consider the possibility that her appearance might upset them.

"*There* you are, Bree," Agnes said. "I've been looking everywhere for you."

"She's been coming here how long," Dusty said to Aubrey, "and hasn't figured out yet that if you aren't in your room or mine, you're either down by the river or in the gazebo?" He tapped his temple. "Is she feeble-minded or senile, or both?"

Head high, Agnes pursed her lips. "I'll just wait in your room, dear, to hear whatever was so critically important that you just *had* to see me this evening."

With that, she turned on her heel and marched down the hall.

"Tell me something," Dusty said.

Aubrey got to her feet and took hold of her walker's handrail.

"How'd somebody as nice as you," he said, pointing toward the door, "come out of *that*?"

124

She was torn between thanking him for the minuscule compliment and defending her mother. "Oh, she isn't all bad, all the time."

"Yeah. Sometimes, she's only half-bad."

On her feet, she ruffled what was left of his hair, and it didn't escape her notice that he smiled. Not much, but he smiled.

As she shuffled toward her room, Aubrey heard the hum of his wheelchair as he turned to face the windows once more.

Funny, she thought, *how standing at the brink of death changes a person.* Six months ago, she would have wished Dusty could hang on indefinitely, in the hope that in a month or a year, researchers would discover a cure for his cancer. Now? Now she hoped that when his will to fight faded, he'd go gently to the other side of the veil.

When Aubrey reached her room, her mother's stiff-backed posture told her the next few minutes wouldn't be easy. Or pleasant. But she plowed ahead, anyway, despite Agnes's pessimism, explaining why it was imperative to be in the mountains, right now, while the woods pulsed with color. For every logical point she cited, Agnes came up with five to shoot it down. She was so busy, in fact, citing reasons *not* to go that she didn't even notice when Aubrey surrendered.

"You know I'd do anything for you, Bree, especially now. But a five-hour drive—each way—to the mountains? Where the weather is unpredictable? In a *camper*?" Agnes shook her head. "It would kill you."

Probably, but wasn't it better to *choose* the ending for her life than to slip quietly into a drug-induced coma, helpless and unable to think or make decisions?

"All right, Mama. You win." She forced a smile. "I appreciate your coming here so late, and we're both exhausted. Let's call it a night, okay?"

Agnes exhaled a sigh of relief. "That's the most sensible thing you've said tonight." She gave Aubrey a quick once-over. "Need any help getting ready for bed?"

"No, I'll be okay, but thanks."

She strode across the room, doled out a hug and a kiss, and said she'd stop by at lunchtime.

Once she was gone, Aubrey breathed a sigh of relief and fell into bed fully clothed. As drowsiness overtook her, she thought of Franco… her last hope.

Chapter Nineteen

FRANCO HAD JUST ROLLED THE WHEELBARROW FROM the shed when the blue jay landed on the still-open door.

It really did seem as though the bird had been following him around the grounds. So he'd spent an hour or so online in the hope of learning more about blue jays: curious and intelligent, they could mimic other birds. Researchers didn't know how they'd earned a reputation for stealing eggs from other nests, because in every study, it was only true about one percent of the time.

Now, the jay did its impersonation of a hawk, and Franco grinned. "Yeah, I'm annoyed by false accusations, too," he said, thinking of the many times Southerners had branded him less than acceptable for no reason other than his New England roots.

"Where have you been lately?" Last time he'd seen the bird, it had flown into one of the towering live oaks out back, disappearing and reappearing in the spooky-looking Spanish moss that draped from the branches, like a kid playing Peek-a-Boo.

The jay answered with a quiet *putt-putt* that came from deep in its throat.

"Ah, got a couple acorns stored in your pouch, do ya?"

The jay lowered its crest slightly—a sign it was at ease, despite Franco's nearness—as if to say, "How'd you know I could do that?"

"Much as I'm enjoying our little visit, I have work to do." He grabbed the wrought-iron handle, intent on closing the door. "So if you don't mind…"

But the bird stayed put.

"Seriously? You *want* me to scare you?"

The crest stood straight up as it calmly pecked at the trim boards. Then it looked at Franco, first with one eye, then with the other, and took off, wings flapping a half dozen time before settling into a long, smooth glide. It was a gorgeous sight against the blue Savannah sky. He wondered if Aubrey had done any paintings of the jay. Maybe later he'd ask her. He'd been wanting to find out what she'd thought of the party, anyway.

Securing the shed door, he headed for the rose garden. This would be their last pruning before he was forced to cut them back and mulch them for the winter. He moved from shrub to shrub, tossing spiky stems and spent blossoms into the wheelbarrow.

"I think your friendship with that blue jay is sweet."

He stepped out from behind the bushes. "Aubrey. Hey. You mean Gilbert?"

"Gilbert…"

"He has a grating voice, like the voice of the duck in those commercials."

She nodded, and her smile brightened her wan face.

"You're lookin' pretty good," he teased, "considering you partied like a college girl day before yesterday."

"Oh, that was something, wasn't it? 'Thank you' seems like such a paltry thing to say to the man who orchestrated it, but thank you, Franco."

It felt good, seeing her this happy. Felt good being the reason for it.

"Why did you leave when you did? I would love to have introduced you to the kids. Even my mom said you were missed."

"I, ah, I met most of 'em on the bus. Before they went up to the solarium." He spotted a slug working its way up a rose branch. Plucking it off, he smashed it between gloved thumb and forefinger, thinking, *I'd rather eat* this *than have another conversation with your mother.* Franco tossed it into the wheelbarrow and said, "I had stuff to do, and it was *your* day, so..." He shrugged.

"What did my mother say to you? Nothing insulting, I hope."

Agnes could insult a person with nothing but a *look.* But that wasn't Aubrey's fault, and she shouldn't carry the guilt for it on her shoulders. Especially not now. "She didn't say anything." *This time.*

"That's a relief. It gets tiresome, apologizing for her insensitive behavior."

"She's just trying to look out for you." Even as he said it, Franco knew that was only partly true. Agnes' behavior benefited Agnes, period. But his words seemed to be what Aubrey needed to hear, and that pleased him.

"I wonder if you have a few minutes to talk."

"We aren't talking now?"

"Well, yes. Of course. But I have something to ask you, and..." She glanced around them, at the residents sitting on the porch just a few feet away, and those pushing walkers toward the gazebo. "... and a little privacy would be nice."

Franco glanced at his watch. By his count, he had six hours of his sentence left to serve. Getting to the end of the punishment as quickly as possible had been the reason he'd skipped breaks, arrived early, and left late these past few days. But what difference would a few minutes make?

He pulled off his work gloves and tucked the pruning shears into his back pocket. "It's nice and shady over there," he said, pointing at a wrought-iron bench across the way. "Will that do?"

She followed his gaze. "It's perfect."

He slowed his pace to match hers. "Did you at least get a piece of cake yesterday?" she asked.

"Yup. Sure did. Got one for Amos, too. It wasn't bad, for store-bought."

"Store-bought is the only kind I've ever eaten."

"Aw, you don't know what you're missing. My wife loved to bake. Jill had this recipe for butter cream frosting…" He grinned at the memory of that last birthday dessert she'd baked for herself, saying, "I hate that greasy stuff they smear all over store-bought cakes."

Aubrey settled onto the bench, and he wondered why she'd chosen the middle, instead of one end or the other.

"So," he said, leaning an elbow on the armrest, "what can I do for you?"

"Do you remember my dream?"

"The one about seeing autumn leaves up north, in person?"

"Yes, that's the one. I know it sounds crazy, but I just *have* to paint them before I die. And I've found the perfect place. I've made all the arrangements. I talked to my mother about taking me there."

"I'm sure it'll be a pleasant trip." *That* was a lie, because he'd Googled 'autumn leaves, Georgia' and knew it would take hours to make the drive to the mountains. Franco couldn't imagine spending that much time with Agnes, cooped up in any vehicle!

"Unfortunately, she said no." On the heels of a sigh, Aubrey added, "She said the trip will kill me."

"I hate to admit it, but she could be right."

"I don't care. I'm already dying. I've had a pretty good life, all things considered, so I don't have many regrets. But *that*?"

Her eyes misted and, hands tightly clasped in her lap, she said, "I'd regret that. A lot. And I can't explain it, either. I know how ridiculous it sounds, but I really don't care."

"You shouldn't have to explain anything." And he meant it.

She touched his knee. "I'm hoping… I'm hoping *you'll* take me, Franco."

They'd been all over this. Franco hated being in this position—saying no to a dying woman?

"I have absolutely no medical training. Heck, I can't even perform CPR."

"You needn't be a doctor or a nurse. You only need to know how to drive."

"But… I lost my license."

"Then you'll just have to obey the rules of the road, so we won't get pulled over."

"I dunno, Aubrey." He slapped a hand to the back of his neck. "It isn't the same as walking you to the gazebo or the solarium."

"I realize what a big imposition this is, but I have every confidence in you. And I trust you." She exhaled a long sigh. "If you can think of another way, I'm open to suggestions."

"What about hiring someone?"

"That would be fine, if all I needed was a ride to the campground. I'll need someone who can stay with me while I paint, too."

He shook his head. "How about a ride share, like in that movie."

"*When Harry Met Sally?*"

"Yeah. They were total strangers when they started out, right?"

"I could never do a thing like that. I'm just not that trusting. Besides, that's the same basic scenario as hiring someone; the person would want to get to their destination, and go their own way, period. Babysitting a terminal cancer patient wouldn't be part of the equation."

"It could be… for the right price."

"Franco, I know my mother has led you to believe that I have more money than the queen of England, but nothing could be further from the truth. I have enough in my savings account to fund this trip and put myself into the ground—so my mother won't have to—and that's about it."

He could think of a dozen reasons to say no, and only one to say yes: making Aubrey's last wish come true.

"*If* I say yes, how long would we be gone?"

"Two, maybe three days at most."

"And when would we leave?"

"Tomorrow."

"Tomorrow! But I'm not supposed to leave the state while I'm still serving my fifty hours. And I hate to be redundant, but Aubrey, my license was suspended."

"You won't need to leave the state. The campground is *in* Georgia. And, much as *I* hate to be redundant, you won't attract the attention of the police if you drive very carefully."

He shook his head. Elbows resting on his knees, Franco leaned forward. "If the cops don't kill me for taking you away from here, your mother will."

"Nothing like that will happen. You'll see. I'll explain everything, and I'll take all the blame."

"I'm not on salary here," he admitted. "You know that, right?"

"It won't cost you a dime. I promise. I've paid for everything in advance—the campground hookups, the RV, maps— and I've withdrawn enough cash to pay for gas and meals, some rudimentary groceries, so no one can track us by my credit card." She squeezed his hand. "I've never begged for anything in my life, but I'll get on my knees—if you'll help me up—and beg you if I have to. Please, Franco, *please* say yes."

"Sheesh, Aubrey." Franco ran a hand through his hair. "You don't believe in making things easy for a guy, do you?"

"I know how hard you're working to get your life back on track. You put in long hours here, and I overheard Amos and Mrs. Kane talking. They said you put in a few hours a week at your old job, too. Have you stopped to consider that this trip might be fun for you, too?"

"No, I can honestly say that never crossed my mind." He took a deep breath, letting it out slowly. "What about your meds? And what if your condition worsens and you need a hospital?"

"Why don't you let me worry about all that?" she asked, patting his knee again.

"Because you have a *brain tumor*, Aubrey, and obviously, you aren't thinking straight." He turned slightly and looked directly into her eyes. "Your mom made a valid point. You really could die during this trip. How am I supposed to deal with—"

"I've written a letter that'll cover all of that. My lawyer has a copy, and once we get to where we're going, I'll give you a copy. That way, if anything happens, you can show it to… whomever… and you'll be in the clear. No one will be able to blame you for anything."

"Except driving without a license. Walking out my community-service obligations." He leaned a little closer to add an emphatic, "*And kidnapping.*"

Aubrey laughed. "Now you're just being melodramatic. And silly. You aren't taking me against my will. If anything, I'm kidnapping *you*!"

She got to her feet. "Trust me on this: I *am* thinking clearly. I doubt I've ever thought about anything more clearly in my entire life. Please, please, *please* say yes."

Franco got to his feet too. Something told him he'd live to regret it, but he said, "Okay."

And before he could say another word, she threw herself into his arms. "Thank you, thank you, *thank you*," she whispered. "I just know there will be a special place reserved for you in heaven for doing this." Leaning back slightly, she added, "I'll be there long before you, so I'll see to it!"

A familiar, high-pitched, nasal voice interrupted them. "Bree! Bree, you get away from that man, this instant, you hear!" Together, they said, "Uh-oh." And together, they laughed.

Chapter Twenty

AUBREY HAD BEEN ASLEEP FOR THREE OF THEIR FIVE hours on the road, and no wonder. The escape—and maneuvering the thirty-seven-foot RV—had probably put *him* five years closer to the grave, so he couldn't imagine how the stress had affected her frail little body.

He glanced over at her, mouth slightly open, chest rising and falling with each shallow breath. *How many more of those,* he wondered, *until she breathed her last?*

If the GPS was correct, they'd arrive at Moccasin Creek State Park in fifteen minutes. He'd give her another ten minutes before waking her to find the reservation confirmation. Franco remembered when she'd said *he* might enjoy the trip as well. Maybe, but not until he'd hooked into the campground's utilities so she'd have the heat and light she'd need. He wanted to check out the path to the lake, and make sure it really was wheelchair accessible, like it said in the brochure. And she hadn't eaten since early that morning, so he needed to make sure she ate something.

By now, the staff would have given Agnes the deliberately vague note Aubrey had propped on the bedside table in her room at Savannah Falls. He winced, just imagining the woman's reaction. It wouldn't matter that Aubrey had asked her not to interfere, not to call the police, not to worry. She'd blame Mrs. Kane. She'd blame the nurses. She'd blame *him* for putting ideas into her daughter's head. Then she'd call the cops, who'd take the frazzled mother at her word—he'd taken advantage of her dying daughter—and they'd issue a BOLO on him.

Fortunately, he and Aubrey wouldn't be all that easy to find, since the campsite she'd researched at Chattahoochee Bend and the one she'd actually reserved at Moccasin Creek were hours apart. But it wouldn't exactly be difficult, either, if the authorities figured out that she'd used an old maiden-name credit card to book the campsite and order a disposable cell phone.

"If you had any sense at all," he muttered to himself, "you'd come up with a convincing story." Something he could rattle off in a sentence or two when the cops finally caught up with them.

"What did you say?" Aubrey asked, stretching.

"We'll be there any minute. You have the confirmation number handy, for check-in?"

She pressed the button to return her seat to the upright position, then dug around in her purse. "How long was I out?"

"Couple hours."

Yawning, she held out the paperwork, and he said, "Won't they want you to sign in, since the campsite is in your name?"

"Don't worry, I'm not so far gone that I didn't take a few things into account."

"A few things…"

"Such as, no way my mother is okay with any of this. Knowing her, she's probably already got the cops chasing down my credit card, but she won't find anything. I made all the arrangements with one I used before I married Michael." She harrumphed. "Oh, she'll figure it out, eventually, but by that time, I'll have my painting of autumn leaves." She paused, tapping a fingertip to her chin. "You know, it won't surprise me a bit if she makes them put one of those tracer things on my cell phone."

"I wouldn't put it past her."

Now she tapped her temple. "Which is precisely why I threw my smartphone into the trash can when we stopped for gas on our way out of Savannah." She gave a nonchalant shrug. "The contract is up for renewal soon anyway, and since I won't live long enough to bother with that..." She showed him an old-fashioned flip phone. "Before we left, I used this one to make all the final arrangements."

Franco repeated her "why bother with that" line in his head. He'd never understand how easily she seemed to have accepted her fate. In her shoes, he'd be a rambling, staggering mess. The world without her would be a decidedly bleaker place, a fact that tugged at his heart a little.

"For a gal dying of a brain tumor," he said, "you're pretty savvy."

"I try," she said, returning his grin.

"You sure you haven't been on the run before? 'Cause you're pretty good at this flee-the-scene stuff."

"I am, aren't I?" Aubrey sobered slightly to add, "Kinda sad, though, that no one will benefit from my shrewdness."

"Hey, what am I, chopped liver?"

"Well, you don't count, because you'll never need an escape plan." She narrowed her eyes. "*Right?*"

He might... if the cops didn't buy the explanation in Aubrey's letter to Agnes.

"Yeah, well, Ms. Shrewd, just keep in mind that no matter how carefully you planned our little adventure—and it's impressive, I'll admit—it'll only throw the cops off for a while. Sooner or later, they'll come up empty. I think you're right about your mother putting two and two together. And that's when she'll put 'em on our trail, using your maiden name."

"Shows what you know," she said with a wink. "The credit card company misspelled my last name, and I never corrected it."

"Oh. Right. *That'll* slow 'em down—for an hour or two."

"Trust me, when you're this close to shaking hands with the Grim Reaper, every nanosecond counts." She punctuated the statement with a merry wink.

How could she be in such good spirits, he wondered, with the Grim Reaper knocking at her door? Well, at least the nap seemed to have done her some good. Not only had it put a little color in her cheeks, but a little extra pep in her voice as well.

"Well, there it is," he said, pointing at the rugged, wooden welcome sign.

Aubrey pulled a long blond wig out of her bag and, peering into the visor mirror, adjusted it as they rolled to a stop at the gate.

A female ranger stepped up to the driver's window, looked over the paperwork, then gave Franco directions to their campsite.

"Think she'll be able to identify me when the Savannah police come calling?"

"No," he said, "but they won't be looking for a gorgeous blond. It's *my* picture they'll show her."

She tossed the wig back into her bag. "You know, I hadn't considered that. But don't worry, I'll make everything right once we get back to Savannah Falls."

Where a SWAT team will be waiting in full riot gear, he told himself, *to haul your skinny—*

"I'm hungry. Are you?"

"Starved," he said, and unhurriedly backed onto their assigned parking slab.

"Then while you're getting us hooked up, I'll make us some sandwiches. We can have a quick lunch, then go exploring."

"Can I ask you a question?" he asked, shifting into park.

"Anything."

"Why did you bring enough food to feed a family of five for a week? You don't eat enough to keep that crazy blue jay friend of yours alive." He narrowed one eye. "Hey, you're not planning to hold me prisoner out here so you'll have more time to paint, are you?"

"For your information, birds eat ten times their weight every day."

Aubrey laughed. It was almost worth a stint at Georgia State Prison to see her so happy.

"Speaking of which," she said, "I've been meaning to talk to you about that bird. He was mine before you came to Savannah Falls, you know. He'd sit in the tree outside my window every morning and every evening, chattering like a chipmunk. Kept me company when I went to the gazebo, too, or sat near the river to paint. I don't mind admitting, I kind of resent that you… that you interloped on our relationship."

He could point out that she hadn't answered his question, could explain that the bird had been a major distraction, annoying him at every turn. Instead, he simply said, "Sorry."

"I named him and everything."

Franco swiveled the driver's seat, then stood and stretched in the cabin. "Oh?"

"Bobbit."

"As in 'Lorena'?"

"No, of course not! I'm sure you noticed that he has this habit of bobbing his head, left and right, up and down." She shrugged. "I was talking to him from my side of the window screen one day, and the name just sort of popped out."

He hit a button, and the door hissed open. "I've been calling him Gilbert."

She wrinkled her nose. "Why?"

"Because when he revs up that squawk box of his, he sounds like Gilbert Gottfried."

"The guy who was the voice of that duck in the insurance commercials?"

"Yup. Now, why don't you head into the back, stretch out, and catch a few zzzz's while I get us hooked up?"

"Because I already had a nap, and I'm not the least bit tired, that's why." She rose slowly from the passenger seat. "Besides, I promised to fix you something to eat."

"You're the boss…" He left her in the galley kitchen, humming as she placed sandwich fixins on the counter. The way she'd been behaving since they left Savannah gave him a pretty good idea what she'd been like before her diagnosis. And Franco wished he'd known her then.

It took him nearly an hour to figure out how to connect all the cords and hoses, and by the time he finished, Franco was feeling pretty good about himself. Getting the RV set up hadn't been an easy feat, especially without an instruction manual. He climbed into the vehicle, fully prepared to brag about that fact when he saw her flip phone on the counter.

His mouth went dry and his palms grew damp, because *his* cell phone was in the RV's cup holder.

Chapter Twenty-One

"I BROUGHT MY BOB ROSS DVDS," SHE SAID AS THEY ATE. "After we eat and take our walk, will you watch them with me?"

"Might as well take advantage of that big flat-screen over there." He used his sandwich as a pointer.

"I thought you were starving."

He glanced at the paper plate, where she'd arranged a ham and cheese sandwich—cut into four tidy sections—with sliced apples and potato chips. So far, he'd managed to make one triangle disappear. She'd gone to so much trouble, covering her tracks, that he felt like a heel saying, "I hate to rain on your parade, but I never gave a thought to *my* cell phone."

Aubrey smirked. "Never fear, Franco dear, because while you were paying for gas at the rest stop, I removed your battery and SIM card."

Good thing he'd already swallowed the bite, because that revelation might have choked him.

"You...you threw 'em *out*?"

"They're easy enough to replace. And not all that expensive, either. Besides, it's high time you put that antique to rest and upgraded to a smartphone."

"It works perfectly fine. I have absolutely no desire to *upgrade*." He shook his head. "*Had* no desire, before you dumped the poor ol' thing." Much as he hated to admit it, her admission relaxed him. The cops would still find them, but without phones or credit cards to pinpoint their location, Aubrey might actually have a couple days to drink in the autumn colors, maybe even get a painting or two completed.

While they ate, Aubrey commented on the RV's interior. "My first apartment wasn't this big. Didn't have granite countertops in the kitchen and bathroom, or tile floors, either."

He considered asking how much a week's rental had set her back, but hey, it was her money and her life—short though it was—so he remained quiet.

When they finished eating, Franco cleared the table and carried her wheelchair outside.

"I don't know why you brought that monstrosity along. I'm *not* sitting in it. I feel fine."

It took a moment to decide whether she was angry or determined. Both, he realized, as she made her way down the steps.

She faltered when her feet hit the pavement, and he reached out to steady her. "Don't be an idiot and use up all your strength in the first hour," Franco said, and scooped her into his arms.

"Normally," she said, wrapping her arms around his neck, "I'd fight you on this. But you're right. If I'm going to get anything accomplished, I need to conserve my energy." She pressed a light kiss to his cheek. "Thanks, Franco, you're probably the best friend I've ever had."

She'd meant every word. He could see gratitude in her eyes and hear it in her voice. It put a lump in his throat, and to mask it, he said, "We won't stay out here long. Wouldn't want you to get a chill."

"My jacket is hanging on the hook beside the door."

He put her down and, when she found her sea legs, he made his way up the RV's steps. Inside, he stood in the tiny entryway and knuckled his eyes. *Better pull yourself together,* he thought. *Time like this, last thing she needs is a sappy wimp at her side.*

He grabbed her coat, and as an afterthought, grabbed her sketch pad and pencil.

"Think we need to lock up?" he asked, helping her into the jacket.

Her eyes were on the path ahead when she said, "No. We won't be gone long. Besides, I have it on good authority that campers are some of the nicest, most honest and helpful people on feet."

"What authority?"

"The RV company's website."

Laughing, he gave in to the urge to pull her into a sideways hug. "You're too much, Aubrey Brewer. Too much."

But her mind was elsewhere—on the shimmering surface of the lake and the hundreds of autumn-leafed trees surrounding it, no doubt. The walk to the pier was short, but the path wasn't smooth. If shifting her weight to maneuver around mounds and shallow holes caused any pain, she gave no sign of it. She spotted a park bench and sat down, head swiveling like a doorknob in an attempt to drink it all in. Franco sat beside her, wishing he could see it through her artistic eyes.

"It's just as I imagined," she whispered, resting her head on his shoulder. "Only a few days ago, I dreamt of a place almost exactly like this. I was walking down a misty path. There was a canopy of trees overhead, and a dear, dear friend at my side..."

Her voice trailed off and, sitting up, she added, "You were much taller in the dream."

Franco forced a grin. "Oh, I was, was I?"

He'd never put much stock in dreams. Why, then, had Aubrey's made a sob ache in his throat?

Two teenage boys in an orange kayak slid by, and in their wake, a middle-aged couple in an aluminum canoe. The husband sent Franco a knowing grin, then winked as he paddled by. Until that moment, Franco hadn't seen himself and Aubrey as a duo. He was nearly old enough to be her dad, after all. He would have been proud to have a daughter like her. She'd accomplished a lot in her forty-some years, and the way she was handling the vicious disease was nothing short of admirable.

A frosty breeze kicked up and she began to shake. He stood, thinking to suggest that they turn back, get out of the wind. That's when he saw that she was crying, not cold. Franco pretended not to notice, and disguised his concern by zipping her jacket all the way to her chin. If anyone had a right to weep, it was Aubrey.

"It's breathtaking," she said quietly, slowly. "So much more beautiful than I imagined. There's no way I can duplicate all this perfection on a canvas."

He used his forefinger to turn her face toward his. "But you have to try. I'm going to *make* you try."

"Many have tried, few have succeeded," she shot back.

But he noticed right away that the music of her voice had ebbed.

"That's enough for one day," he said, taking her arm. "We'll rest up, have a good supper and a good night's sleep, and come back in the morning. Weather report says it'll be warmer. Besides, who knows how great this place will look in the morning light."

After an hour or so huddled under a multi-colored afghan, dozing to the soothing voice of Bob Ross—who painted happy mountains and footpaths across the TV screen— Aubrey placed her easel near the big reclining seat at the front of the RV, and spent another hour working on Dusty's painting.

"I've made a decision," she said. "I'm not going to duplicate his family's sailboat. I'm going to paint him here, sitting by the lake, surrounded by autumn color."

"That's a great idea."

But she hadn't heard him, because already she'd lost herself in the work. Franco sat, content to watch her add details—a spark in the boy's eyes, a slight upturn to one corner of his mouth, a lock of hair falling across his forehead—and marveled at her talent.

"You're really good, but I guess you already know that."

"My work is just passable when compared to the greats. Rembrandt. Picasso. Gauguin."

"Do you have a favorite artist? One you've tried to emulate?"

"Oh, that's easy," she said, brow furrowing and squinting as she highlighted a lock of hair, "Van Gogh, hands down."

"Yeah. He's pretty cool. I've always thought he was nearsighted."

Aubrey met his eyes. "Nearsighted?"

"When I wasn't wearing my glasses, things looked a whole lot like they do in his paintings."

"I've never seen you in glasses."

"That's because I had laser eye surgery several years back."

"I imagine you looked very collegiate. Let me guess... black horn-rimmed frames, like Buddy Holly?"

"Nope. Silver wire. And round."

"Wow. John Lennon, huh? When I'm wrong, I'm wrong."

Normally, Franco didn't like idle chitchat. But with Aubrey, it felt comfortable, felt *right,* almost the way it had with Jill.

Almost.

"So what are you in the mood for tonight? Grilled cheese and tomato soup, or tuna patties with mac and cheese?"

"I'm not hun—"

"The question isn't *if* you'll eat, it's *what.*"

Aubrey rolled her eyes. "All right. Fine... Dad."

"Hey. If you're gonna act like a child, I have no problem treating you like one." He stared her down. "So? Which is it gonna be? Grilled cheese or tuna patties?"

"What's that old saying? 'Try something new before you die'? I've probably had a couple hundred grilled cheese sandwiches."

He had read that cops often use dark humor to take the edge off on-the-job horrors. Evidently, Aubrey's morbid end-of-life comments helped her cope with the inevitable. Unfortunately, he'd never developed such skills.

While he pulled the meal together, she huddled under a blanket, the Bob Ross book he'd given her open on her lap. But she wasn't reading. Instead, she'd dozed off.

No surprise there. Her first day of freedom was coming to an end. Franco chopped vegetables for the salad, and decided that the best course of action was to get her fed and put to bed. She had a day, two at most, he acknowledged, before Agnes sicced the cops on them. Time was slipping away, literally, and he'd feel like a first-class heel if he let her die without realizing her dream.

At the word *die*, he nearly lopped off a fingertip. But there was no dodging it. Every passing hour made that more evident. Her fair skin seemed translucent now, and her movements were sluggish. She'd tried her best to hide it, but Franco could tell that each breath came with effort. For now, thankfully, sleep had delivered Aubrey some much-needed relief from the pain ... and thinking about the inevitable end.

They hadn't talked much about that, partly because she'd never volunteered any information about what she was going through, physically, and partly because he hadn't had the heart to ask. She looked so peaceful and content, snuggled up on the couch, that he hated to disturb her. But she had to get some food into her stomach, or the anticholinergic prescribed to avert dizziness would have her up all night, heaving.

"Hey, kiddo," he said, giving her shoulder a gentle shake. "Soup's on."

He could see that it was a struggle, just opening her eyes. He'd never been big on prayer. If he could take a knee without rousing her suspicion, he'd do it, right there in front of the couch. *Give her a few days to paint those trees... then I'll get her back to Savannah Falls, where she'll be safe until...*

Tears stung his eyes, and Franco straightened and put his back to her so she wouldn't see them. *And when it's time, Lord, take her fast and easy.*

She pulled herself up on one elbow, wincing slightly at the effort. "Something smells delicious."

He held out his forearm, and when she took hold of it, Franco helped her to her feet. The distance between the couch and the table was two yards, tops. Yet by the time she slid into the booth, Aubrey was out of breath. Was he man enough to watch her slip away, breath by breath?

She talked a blue streak as they ate, detailing how she'd place Dusty in a canoe, similar to the one the older couple had paddled past them earlier. "I'll make sure the sky is the bluest blue, with a few cumulus clouds hovering overhead. I'll muss up his hair, just a tad, to give the indication that there's a slight breeze on the lake." She slurped up a spoonful of soup. "This isn't like any canned tomato soup I've ever had. What did you do to it?"

"Added a pat of butter, some salt and pepper, and a pinch of sugar."

"Well, it's delicious." She swallowed another taste. "Is that the way your mom used to make it?"

"No. That was Jill's recipe... if you want to call it that."

Funny how talking about her with Aubrey made him miss her less. And differently. It was as though by encouraging him to remember the little niceties, he'd finally started to heal.

"Don't look that way," she said.

"What way?"

"All... regretful, as though you're sorry you survived when she didn't."

Franco speared a forkful of the tuna patty. This wasn't a subject he cared to discuss. Not now. Not ever. Not even with Aubrey.

"You loved her a lot, huh."

"Yeah. She was by far the best thing that ever happened to me."

"And you miss her like crazy, don't you?"

"Oh, only every minute of every day." But thanks to Aubrey, missing Jill didn't hurt the way it once had.

"You think she'd be happy, knowing that you're beating yourself up over it?"

"What do you mean?"

"The accident wasn't your fault, and neither was her death. I'm sure Jill would be quick to point out that you shouldn't feel guilty for surviving, even though she didn't."

"Look. Aubrey. No disrespect intended, but what did or didn't happen—what I do or do not feel—is none of your business."

Blinking and wide-eyed, she only stared at him. And oh, what he wouldn't give to have mind-reading powers in that moment.

"Hmm, let me guess. You picked a fight over something nonsensical, took your eyes off the road for a split second and—"

Franco didn't know how much more of this he could stand. Not without lashing out at her, anyway. And what kind of coldhearted fool would he be if he did that?

"It is what it is, y'know?"

She rolled her eyes. "I hate that saying."

"Why?"

"It smacks of avoidance, and I've always believed in meeting problems head-on."

"Yeah, well, not everyone is as strong or as sane as you are, Aubrey."

Hands up in surrender, she shrugged. "All right. Okay. You don't have to hit me in the head with a brick. I can take a hint." *Coulda fooled me.*

"Oh my goodness!" she said, sitting taller at the table. "There's a blue jay in the shrub outside the window, and he looks just like Bobbit!"

Close, but no cigar, he thought. That bird didn't have a split crest. And something told him that even if a pane of glass hadn't separated them, it wouldn't have made eye contact. Or dive-bombed him.

"I hope he'll be all right after…"

After she was gone? "Why wouldn't he be?"

"Because I've made sure Amos has plenty of black-oil sunflower seeds to scatter around. Jays mostly eat bugs and grubs, but Bobbit loves the stuff. I think that's why his feathers are bluer than the rest of his clan."

"His clan." Franco snickered. "So, like, when he isn't buggin' me, he puts on a kilt and breaks into a Highland dance?"

She rolled her eyes. "Oh. You're such a riot."

"Sarcasm doesn't become you."

"Yeah, well…" Her voice trailed off as she realized the jay had taken off. Aubrey put down her spoon and leaned both elbows on the table. "Franco?"

"Yeah?"

"Promise me something?"

"What?"

"When you finish up your fifty hours, give some serious thought to auditioning at the comedy club. Because it'd be a big fat shame to waste all that funny stuff on tow truck customers."

"Yeah, well," he copied, "for your information, I'm giving serious thought to saving my money, maybe enrolling in some night classes. A two-birds-with-one-stone kinda thing: while I'm working on my horticulture certificate, I won't be as tempted to hit the bars."

He saw a faint spark in her blue eyes.

"Way to go, Franco Allessi, way to go!" She high-fived him, then gave his hand an enthusiastic pat. "You have a real

149

knack for the work, and I know at least one rose bush that would agree. You saved that poor little thing's life!"

He pictured the stubborn hybrid shrub, growing leggy and pale when he'd arrived at the hospice center. He'd given it all he had: fertilizer, mulch, pruning, spritzing. He'd even transplanted it, thinking the problem was in the soil. And in the past week or so, he'd noticed buds, proof that it would flower again. With any luck, Aubrey might see it bloom before—

"Supper was delicious," she said, interrupting his thoughts, "but I'm not very hungry."

"So?"

"So… I don't feel like eating."

He took her fork and moved a few green beans and bites of tuna to the edge of her plate. "Just try and get that little bit down. You can't take your meds on an empty stomach. And you need the meds. You said yourself that without them, you won't be able to hold the paintbrush steady. Besides, you'll sleep better with a full belly."

Aubrey took a breath, gearing up to fire off a list of reasons for saying no. When she didn't, he crossed both arms over his chest. "Looking forward to tomorrow, when you can get back outside and finish the painting?"

One eyebrow rose slightly. "Finish it? It'll probably take longer than a day. Everything will depend on how well things come together. Light. Shadows." She grinned. "My *muse*, if you will. Painting isn't an exact science, you know."

"Sounds time-consuming, so you'd better eat something, or you won't last an hour out there."

Aubrey matched his gaze, blink for steady blink, then exhaled a raspy sigh… and took a bite. "You're almost as bad as my mother."

Franco started to disagree, but thought better of it. For one thing, why remind her of her mother's controlling behavior? For another, if he hoped to help make her dream come true, he needed her full cooperation, and insulting her mom was no way to get it.

"Want me to put something on TV for you while I do the dishes?"

She glanced toward the couch, where her blanket still lay in a rumpled heap. "Would you think I'm the rudest person ever if I just went to bed?"

"Are you kidding? I think that's a great idea." He got up and started down the hall. "Let me make sure you'll have everything you need, and grab some bedding for myself." Aiming a forefinger in her direction, he said, "You stay put until I get back. I'll do the dishes later."

"I'm not an invalid, you know."

But you might be safer if you were. "Why risk another dizzy spell and clunking your head or something?"

"*Another* dizzy spell?"

"Thought I didn't notice, huh? I'm a recovering alcoholic. I know woozy when I see it."

He didn't give her time to say more. In the bedroom, he made up the king-sized bed, then checked to see that towels, soap, and the bathmat were in easy reach near the sink and shower. Earlier, he'd tossed their duffel bags into the closet. Now, unzipping hers, he dug around until he found a white sweatsuit and thick white socks. Could she get out of her outfit and into this stuff, all by herself? *Only one way to find out.*

Stacking sheets, a blanket and pillow in his arms, he returned to the RV's living area.

"I laid out your night clothes," he said, putting his linens on the far end of the couch. "But I have a question for you."

She looked tired—of answering questions, of being awake, of facing death.

"Will you let me help you change?"

"I'll manage." Aubrey rose slowly... and nearly lost her footing.

"That does it."

Franco picked her up, carried her to the bedroom, and deposited her on the bed. Down on one knee, he removed her shoes and socks and, rolling her from one side to the other, tugged off her jeans. She felt like a rag doll as he slid the sweatpants over her hips. It was as he pulled on the clean socks that he looked up, into her tear-streaked face.

Sitting on the edge of the mattress beside her, Franco pulled her close. "Aw, honey, I'm sorry. I shouldn't have been in such a rush. I didn't mean to be so rough. Did I hurt you?"

"No," she said, her voice little-girl squeaky. "I just… I just *hate* being so dependent."

Franco cupped her face in his hands, thumb pads drying her tears as he said, "Don't think of it that way. You're sick. You'd do it for me if things were reversed, right?"

She nodded, and he pressed a brotherly kiss to her forehead. "Besides, this is good for me."

A tiny giggle popped from her lips. "Good for you? How do you figure *that*?"

"I've never taken care of anyone, not once in my whole life."

"What?" She studied his face. "But Franco… you were married. For *two decades*!"

"Yeah, and Jill spoiled me rotten. I did my share of work on the job, but she did everything else. Took me months after the accident to figure out how to do the most rudimentary stuff—laundry, grocery shopping, running the vacuum, loading the dishwasher." He grinned a little, thinking of how filthy he'd let the trailer get before Aubrey's painting had inspired him to clean up. "First time I changed our bed, took me over an hour. I got so sweaty and out of breath, fighting with that fitted sheet, I needed a shower afterward."

Aubrey smiled. "What about your parents? Are they still alive?"

"Yeah. They're still toughing out the cold winters in New Hampshire." He hung his head. "Haven't seen them since about six months after Jill's funeral, though. All they could talk about was my drinking, not Jill, not the accident, not what my plans were. So I told 'em to go home." He exhaled a ragged sigh. "And they did."

She made an *"oh well"* face. "What about brothers and sisters?"

"Had a brother. I was twelve when we lost him."

Aubrey leaned into him, and he slid his arms around her.

"I'm sorry," she said. "I didn't mean to open old wounds."

What she didn't know—what he couldn't explain—was that the wounds had never healed to begin with. Losing Tony wasn't something he talked much about, not even to Jill. And yet Franco heard himself say, "He played defensive end for the high school football team, and I never missed a home game. The day it happened, the guys were just coming back onto the field after halftime. Tony was walking along the sidelines, snapping his helmet's chin strap, and… and he went down like a felled tree."

"He was tackled? On the sidelines?"

"No. Tony was one of those people born with coronary abnormalities. The arteries aren't connected like they're supposed to be, and sometimes, exercise can leave them compressed. So basically, he died because he wasn't getting enough blood to his heart."

"Oh my," she whispered. "How awful for you. For your folks too. How old was he?"

"Just shy of his sixteenth birthday."

For a long moment, Aubrey sat quietly. Then she sat back, slid both arms out of her sleeves and tucked them under her shirt. And, just as a magician plucks silk scarves from his pocket, she produced a lacy pink bra and sling-shotted it across the room.

"Jill used to do that. If I live to be a thousand, I'll never figure out *how.*"

"Trade secret," she said with a wink. "So when are you going to fix things with your folks?" she asked, sliding her arms back into the shirt sleeves. "Life is short." Arms akimbo, she added, "Here sits proof of that."

Franco was still trying to puzzle out the trick when she added, "How old are your parents?"

"Mid-70s." When they'd driven down for the wake and funeral, they were still doing crazy things—playing golf, hiking, traveling to places like Patagonia and Palau. But Tony had been young and healthy when his heart condition killed him, so—

"The longer you wait to make contact, the more difficult it'll be."

Hard to argue with the logic of that. And yet…

"Promise me you'll do it, first chance you get."

He'd made and kept just one promise in his life—to Jill, on their wedding day, and saw no reason to make another one now.

Chapter Twenty-Two

FRANCO SPRAWLED ON THE COUCH, FLICKING THROUGH the channels. He'd muted the television, thinking that if he found something worth watching, he'd put it at a volume that wouldn't disturb Aubrey. He'd had plenty of practice, watching TV this way after Jill turned in for the night. His mom did the same thing, staying up most nights long after his dad had turned in. A simple matter of one person needing more sleep than the other? Or a means of escape, a way to claim some time and privacy in an always there living arrangement?

He toed off his shoes, flinching slightly as each thumped to the carpet. He crossed one ankle over the other and heard Aubrey moan softly in her sleep. The last half-dozen times, he'd jumped up, raced down the hall and stood beside the bed, watching and listening until he was sure everything was all right. She'd been in pain, no doubt, but alive. How many more nights did she have left, he wondered now. How many sunrises? A dozen? Two, if she was lucky?

He issued a groan of his own and sat up. Elbows on knees and head in his hands, he uttered a string of obscenities at the injustice of it all. On his feet now, he paced the small space between the banquette and the sofa. He slapped a hand to the back of his neck and ground his molars together. Why did good people like Tony and Jill and Aubrey have to die of stupid, unnecessary things like heart failure, accidents, and cancer, while others—whose every breath was a waste of oxygen— enjoyed long, healthy lives?

"There's something wrong about that," he muttered. "Really wrong."

Suddenly, the roomy RV felt like a coffin. He needed fresh air and space, and threw open the door. Oh, what he wouldn't give for a cigarette right now. And two fingers of Kentucky bourbon. No, three fingers. He licked his lips and swallowed. Hard. Good thing he didn't have access to keys and a car, because…

He sat on the wooden picnic table and, feet planted on its bench, Franco looked around at the rainbow glow of colored lanterns, strung between the trees at a nearby campsite, at the flicker of a bonfire across the way. Around the bend in the road, kids laughed and squealed as their flashlights' strobes flicked up, down, back, and forth in search of the ever-elusive Snipe. The moon hung low in the sky, its silver-white light turning the mica-laced gravel parking lot into a blanket of minuscule diamonds, and painted tree-shadows that wrapped around the RV like hideous witch fingers. The wind picked up, whirling dried leaves into mini-tornadoes that skipped and bounced over the ground, then disappeared beneath cars and campers. Hunching his shoulders into it, Franco shivered a bit.

Better knock it off, he thought, *you're scaring yourself.*

Soft music—something by the Eagles, unless he was mistaken—filtered across the campground and calmed him. The breeze lifted his frosty breaths and carried them away. Things were just way too normal and serene, especially considering that inside, with every inhalation and exhalation, Aubrey moved one breath closer to the end of her life.

On his feet now, he pocketed his hands and circled the wooden table. *Should have put your shoes on,* he thought as gravel poked through his socks. The discomfort reminded him of an article he'd read, claiming that chemo left some cancer patients with neuropathy in their hands and feet, making every step an uncertain venture. He'd never thought to ask Aubrey if nerve damage was responsible for her slow, halting pace.

The need to do something for her hit hard. Franco wanted to bellow into the cold black sky, "If you're really up there, why don't *You* do something!" Instead, he continued pacing. "If wishes were fishes," his mom liked to say, "we'd all cast nets."

Yawning into a fist, he headed back inside, poured himself a glass of milk, then tiptoed down the hall to check on Aubrey. She'd rolled onto her side, so he couldn't see her face, but her snoring told him she was still with him. Grinning a bit, he decided that tomorrow, first chance she gave him, he'd tease her about that. And if she didn't provide an opening? He'd just blurt out, "Who would've thought a little slip of a thing like you could snore like a chainsaw?"

He downed the milk, rinsed the glass and put it rim-down in the sink. Lights out and TV off, he stretched out on the couch. According to the bright blue numerals of the DVD clock, it was nearly two in the morning. He probably wouldn't sleep. Not with one ear cocked toward the bedroom and his mind swirling with thoughts of Tony and Jill, and his mom and dad.

The scent of fresh-brewed coffee roused him. It took a couple seconds to get his bearings. When he remembered where he was—and why—Aubrey came immediately to mind. He sat up, and found her watching him.

"Sheesh. I thought you'd never wake up."

Unless she'd been faking all those times he'd checked, Aubrey had slept nearly twelve hours. *Sure doesn't look it,* he thought, taking note of the dark hollows beneath her eyes.

He grabbed a mug from the cabinet above the coffee pot.

"How long have you been up?"

"Long enough to know that you chew in your sleep."

"Oh yeah? Well, you snore."

"I do not!"

Lifting a shoulder, Franco said, "Sorry. But yes, you do. I half expected the people at the next campsite to come over here to find out why we were sawing logs in the middle of the night."

She ignored the slur and wrinkled her nose. "You drink your coffee black?"

He grimaced at her cup—mostly milk and, if he had to guess, two spoonfuls of sugar. "I used to drink mine that way… when I was *ten*."

Aubrey rolled her eyes. "Can I help it if I like sweet things?"

"Ah. So that explains it, then."

One eyebrow rose on her forehead.

"Why you like me so much."

Giggling, she shook her head. "Yeah. That must be it."

"Had breakfast yet?"

"Nope. But then, I never eat breakfast."

"I make a mean omelet." He got up. "I'm making one, and you're eating some of it."

"I'm not, and you can't make me."

"I can, and I will." He slid the egg carton and cheese out of the fridge. "You'll have breakfast and take your meds, or I'll turn this bus around and drive you straight back to Savannah Falls."

Her eyes widened. "You wouldn't."

His eyes narrowed. "Try me."

Aubrey tucked in one corner of her mouth, then exhaled a sigh.

"What time did you go to sleep?" she asked.

"I dunno. Two, two-thirty?"

"Well, that explains your sour mood."

Franco cracked three eggs into a bowl, fork-whipped them into a froth and said, "You like cheese on your omelets?"

"Sure. Why not."

"Sausage or bacon?"

"Greasy stuff makes me queasy these days, so if it's all right with you, *Da-a-d,* neither."

Last night, he'd wondered whether she or her husband had been the go-to-bed-early partner. He'd given up gambling when he quit drinking, but he had a feeling that putting his money on Aubrey was a safe bet. He'd also bet that before cancer, she'd probably been what his dad called "a live wire." The phrase made him grin to himself, because even now— ravaged by cancer—she was a force to be reckoned with.

She topped off her coffee, and Franco couldn't help but notice that her hands were shaking.

"Take your meds yet?"

"Soon as I eat," she promised. "And don't give me that 'I'll believe it when I see it' look. I want to be steady when I get out there to paint."

He peered out the window above the sink. "Kinda breezy out there. Good thing you have a turtleneck."

Turning to see why she hadn't responded with, "I do not have a turtleneck," he saw that she'd leaned into the corner of the booth and dozed off. "Too bad," he said to himself. Because he had a feeling the comeback would have been a mind bender.

She slept as he set the table, as he whisked the eggs and they sputtered and popped in the frying pan, as he loaded the toaster with whole wheat bread. He was about to pour two glasses of orange juice when he remembered another article he'd read, about how cancer drugs caused mouth ulcers, and acidic foods and drinks irritated them. He filled two tumblers with milk instead.

The toast popped up, startling her awake.

"Ack," she said, stretching. "I don't have curtain wrinkles on my cheek, do I?"

He sliced off a small tip of the omelet, plated it, and slid it in front of her. "I didn't butter your toast," he said. "Wasn't sure if you could, ah—pardon the pun—stomach it."

A crooked smile lit her face. "You're too good to me." She wasn't kidding.

"Go on, give it a try."

She took a bite of the omelet.

"How is it?"

"You want the truth? Or should I pretend?" That took him by surprise, and he said so.

"I can't taste much of anything, thanks to the chemo."

"But… you haven't had a treatment in, what, months?"

"The stuff sticks with you. Because it's poison. Literally. Oh, sure, it kills some cancer cells, but it kills other things, too. Like taste and smell. The feeling in your fingertips and toes. Changes your heartbeat. Gives you bad breath."

She brightened and sang, "Every breath you take…"

He joined in with, "Every move you make…"

And they harmonized, "I'll be watching you."

"Hey, we're pretty good together."

"I couldn't agree more. Never had a girl friend before." Her eyebrows rose.

"Not a girlfriend, goofball. A girl *friend.*" He winked. "Guess there's a first time for everything."

She finished her portion of the omelet. "So," she said, drawing an imaginary line in the air around him, "you sleep in your clothes all the time? Or just when you're worried someone might die on your watch?"

"Jeez, Aubrey, I suppose I get why you say stuff like that, but man. I wouldn't complain if you did it *less.*"

Reaching across the table, she patted his hand. "I'm sorry. Honest. I'll reel it in a little."

"Good. Thanks. And to answer your question, I sleep in my clothes a lot. Mostly because I fall asleep in front of the TV. A lot."

She propped her chin on a fist. "Oh? You have a favorite show?"

"Sorta. It's called 'Surf the Channels.'"

"You're hilarious. Remember. After I'm gone: comedy club. You'll leave 'em rollin' in the aisles."

"If you expect me to believe that, you could at least fake a smile."

"Oh. Right. I guess that did come out a tad insincere, didn't it." She showed every tooth in her head, then said, "Better?"

"I guess... if you're auditioning for a part in a zombie movie."

Aubrey laughed. "See? Now that's funny stuff!"

Franco finished his breakfast and carried their plates to the counter.

"Better run water on those," she said. "When eggs dry, they're like cement."

Chitchat? Again? When she could die at any moment? He filled the sink, and looked over his shoulder to say, "You need help getting ready?"

Her smile vanished, like smoke from a spent match. "I don't know." She struggled to get to her feet. "Maybe. I hope not."

"Well, if you need a hand..." He extended his, palm up.

Aubrey stepped up to him. "I know." She gave him what for her, at least, was a fierce hug.

As she hobbled down the hall, he stood, ready to race down there if she looked the least bit unsteady. Fortunately, she made it without aid. Unfortunately, she closed the door. Not a great idea, since it would muffle any sounds of distress and waste precious seconds if he needed to get in to help her.

Ten minutes later, he'd finished the dishes and laced up his running shoes, and still no sign of Aubrey. He understood that, in her condition, it took longer to do everything. If she hadn't said straight out how much she hated being dependent...

"Hey Aubrey," he hollered. "Need a hand with anything?"

A second ticked by, then two. "I'm okay," she said at last. "I'll be out in a minute, but I'll need help with my shoes."

Standing outside the door, he said, "Are you decent?"

He heard a soft laugh, followed by, "Physically or mentally?"

Chuckling, Franco opened the door and picked up her shoes. "Here. Hold these," he said, lifting her. Just as he was about to put her down on the couch, Aubrey ran a finger across his brow.

"Guess it was a bad idea, making me eat all that food." She glanced at her fingertip, then showed him the glistening tip. "Hefting my bulk around has made you perspire."

"Bulk. Right." Franco grabbed the finger, gave it an affectionate squeeze. "And you say I'm the comedian."

"What I said wasn't funny."

"Yeah, I know. That's why I'm the comic and you're—"

"—the straight man," they said together.

"We make a good team," she said.

"A really good team," he agreed.

He hoped he had the strength of character to stay clean and sober when she was gone, because losing her was going to hurt like crazy.

Chapter Twenty-Three

WHEN AUBREY FOUGHT HIM ABOUT USING THE wheelchair, he'd played the "I'll take you back home" card again. And again, it worked. How did she feel about the decision now, he wondered, after seeing how far it was from the RV to the lakeside?

"You warm enough?" he asked.

"You've got me bundled up like Nanook of the North. I'll be lucky if I can lift my arm, let alone bend it enough to hold a paintbrush."

"Hmpf," he said. "But are you warm enough?"

Aubrey laughed quietly. "Oh, you know me so well. Yes. I'm fine."

As they neared the shore, he stopped. "See anything that looks paintable from here?"

She scanned the beach, then pointed. "Oh, look at the way the light comes through the trees over there," she said, her voice a near whisper. "Do you think the path goes that far?"

He followed her line of sight. "Stay put," he said, braking the chair, "and I'll find out."

Franco jogged in the direction she'd pointed, stopping where the boardwalk blended into the shin-deep grass. He guessed twenty, maybe thirty yards between here and the spot she'd chosen. Thirty yards of hilly, uneven ground. If he tried to push the chair that far, she'd pass out from the pain... or worse. And carrying her would be almost as bad. Waving to get her attention, he lifted his arms in a gesture of helplessness.

He jogged back and squatted in front of the chair. "It's a big lake. Must be a couple thousand trees. Surely there's something closer."

A flicker of disappointment flashed across her face, but she quickly hid it behind a smile. "I don't suppose there's a rabbit's foot on your keychain..."

Franco got the joke and patted his pockets. "Sorry."

A sigh of disappointment passed her lips, and then she winked. "We're burnin' daylight, cowboy. Giddy-yup."

When they reached the new spot, Franco set up her easel and Aubrey talked nonstop about the interplay of light and shadow, the reflection of trees in the water, the balance of space—between the treetops and the sky, among the trees themselves. But Franco was too distracted to pay full attention: how would she reach the canvas while seated? An idea took shape as he set up the small camp stools. Opening her paint kit, he placed it on the nearest one.

"Hey! What are you doing in there? I've got everything organized just the way I like—"

"I'm hoping you have a palette knife in here."
She leaned forward and grabbed two.

Franco tested the strength of the handles, and chose the largest. "This'll do," he said, and proceeded to drill four holes in the sandy soil.

"Franco! I paid thirty bucks each for those things!"

"Don't worry." He wiped it on his jeans and handed it back. "See? It's fine." Next, he dropped the easel's legs into the holes. "There," he said, rolling the chair closer. "I can lower it if it's still too high. Or raise it if it's too low."

Aubrey put both hands on the utensil tray. "No, this is nice. Really nice." She smiled up at him. "You're kinda remarkable, you know that?"

He slid the art kit closer, then clamped her canvas in place. "Good?"

"Great. No, better than great. Amazing." A tiny gasp escaped her lips. "I just thought of the perfect stage name for you!"

"Stage name? What—"

"You know, for when you give up tow-trucking and become a comic." Drawing quote marks in the air, she said, "'The Amazing Franco.'"

"Sounds like a magician, not a comedian."

"You *are* a magician of sorts." Hands out Vanna White-style, she said, "I offer as evidence this just-the-right-height easel. And the poor little rose bush at the hospice center. I could go on, but you get my drift."

"That wasn't magic, it was…" He crossed both arms over his chest. "Say, what's with all this chitchat? Why are you stalling?"

She rummaged in her kit and withdrew a pencil. "Stalling? Who, me?"

"Are you worried the meds won't control your trembling, and that your muse won't materialize *there*?" He tapped a corner of the canvas.

She thumped herself in the forehead. "You're a plant, aren't you, sent to the hospice by my mother to psychoanalyze me."

While she squirted dollops of paint onto her palette, Franco picked up her MP3 player and scrolled through the saved tunes. "Well, what do you know? The artist is an Eagles fan, too." He chose an album and hit play. "Unless you prefer Brahms."

"The lullaby guy? No way. I don't want to sleep. Not ever again. For the rest of my life."

He winced, and she saw it.

"Sorry. That just sort of slipped out. Am I forgiven?"

"We'll see." He picked up the pencil she'd placed in the easel's tray. "So what's this for? You sketch stuff out before you paint?"

"Sometimes I scrape paint from the canvas with the tip. You know, to give the illusion of individual blades of grass, or hair, if I'm doing a portrait." She dipped a brush into gesso and primed the canvas. "But mostly, I use it to tap."

"Tap?"

"You know how some people drum their fingers, or nod, or pace when they're thinking? Well, when I get stuck, blending colors or whatever, I sit back to think about it, and—"

"—tap," they said together.

"Will it bug you if I watch?"

"It'd bug me if you didn't."

Franco sat quietly for several hours, watching as a vibrant autumn scene began to rise from the canvas.

"I don't blame you for being bored," she said, without looking away from her work.

"I'm not bored."

"Sleeping, then?"

"No. Why?"

"It isn't like you to go this long without saying anything."

"Watching you is mesmerizing. I don't want to interrupt."

"Mesmerized. That's how I feel watching Bob Ross DVDs."

"He's good, no doubt about it. But in his case, it's the voice that's hypnotic. In your case, it's… it's like those brushes are magic wands, and you've cast a spell on me."

Her bristle tips hovered over the canvas as she turned to study his face. "Wow. You're serious. I would have bet my easel you were pulling my leg."

"Hey. You know me. I tell it like it is, every chance I get. Besides, your balance is precarious enough without anyone pulling your leg."

Smiling, she groaned and went back to work on the reeds and cattails sprouting from the loamy bank.

"Those students of yours are lucky, having you for a teacher."

"Were lucky, you mean."

"Semantics. Bet if you pretend I'm one of your students, I could actually learn a thing or two about art."

"You underestimate yourself, m'friend. A man who waxes poetic the way you do? Trust me. With a little guidance, you could transport what's in your heart and mind onto canvas. If you had a mind to, that is."

He sat up straighter. Back in high school, he'd taken an art class for no reason other than to fill his electives quota. But he'd enjoyed it, especially when the instructor praised his work.

"I'm sure you've seen YouTube videos of elephants and apes, dolphins and rhinos, even dogs and cats, painting." She snickered. "They're not very good, but they can do it."

"If that's your idea of an incentive..."

She launched into a so-so Julia Child imitation: "First, we begin with a description of subject matter. In this case, of course, autumn leaves. Next, we look closely to see what relationship the subjects have to one another. Then, we describe the colors. How many are used? Are they bright or dark? Is there more movement on one side of the canvas than the other? What's the most important part of the scene... where did your eyes go first? What's the mood of the work? What *feelings* did it bring out in you?"

Aubrey looked over at him. "Oh. You're still awake?"

Her pale skin had taken on a slightly gray pallor, and the shadows under her eyes were a shade darker now. It seemed a struggle to raise her arm, to blend colors or load her brushes, to work the paint into the canvas. But Aubrey, being Aubrey, pressed on.

"You got far more done that I expected. What-say we call this a wrap and head inside."

"I was hoping to put more detail into Dusty's face and hands, in the fabric of his clothing."

167

She looked as disappointed as she sounded, and yet Franco expected her to insist on staying, if only a little longer. Even in her condition, Aubrey could be a powerhouse when she put her mind to it. If he didn't come up with something believable, she'd never agree to get out of this frosty autumn wind.

"I'm tired and hungry and cold," he said. And it wasn't entirely untrue.

"I'll be fine out here alone for a few minutes. Go on back to the RV to grab a jacket and a sandwich."

In addition to her paint kit, easel, and canvas, Franco had tucked a small cooler into the bag on the back of the chair. There was plenty to eat, right here, but she was in no condition—and this wasn't the time or place—for a picnic lunch.

"You want to come back out here tomorrow, don't you?"

She looked at him as if he'd grown a big hairy mole right between his eyebrows. "Of course I do. The whole point of this trip was—"

"You're tired. Don't bother denying it, because it shows in a dozen different ways. If you overdo it today, you won't have the strength tomorrow to pick up where you left off today." He tucked paints into the tube-shaped compartments in her kit. He found a rag, soaked it with mineral spirits, and carefully cleaned the fan brush.

"I'm not kidding," he said as he worked.

"I can see that."

"What's this one called?" he asked, holding up a thick, rounded brush.

"A mop."

"And this?" Franco pointed at the odd-shaped brush, still in her hand.

"Filbert."

Flat, round, bright, and rigger brushes each got a thorough cleaning before he returned them to the suede-lined loops that held them in place on the underside of the kit's lid.

"How do we save the paint on here?" he asked, holding up the palette.

"We don't. The colors change if they dry out, even a little."

Franco ignored her compliant tone. "So that's why you were so stingy with those little blobs."

He wiped the pallet clean, then gave it a once-over with the spirits-soaked rag while Aubrey watched him pack everything up. It scared him, seeing her so weak that she couldn't even muster the energy to give him a hard time for calling her stingy. Regret swelled up inside him, and to keep her from reading his face, Franco focused on the job at hand.

"What're you in the mood for tonight? Caesar salad? Soup? Ice cream sundae?"

She brightened a bit at the mention of that last one.

"Sundae it is, then." He'd found a pamphlet tucked into her art kit, and while she worked, Franco had leafed through it. Palliative care, it explained, shifted the focus from doing everything possible to keep patients *alive* to doing every possible to keep them living *well*.

He did his best to avoid uneven boards as they rolled back to the camper. The trip took all of five minutes, yet Aubrey was fast asleep when he braked the wheelchair near the steps. A storm was rolling in, churning up dark clouds and cold wind, or he might have let her snooze while he hauled everything inside.

"Hey, lazybones," he said, sliding one arm under her knees, the other behind her back. "Let's get you inside before the skies open up."

She nodded.

He gathered her close, then realized he'd forgotten to open the door. It wasn't easy, but he managed without putting her down.

"Guess what they say is true."

"What who says about what?"

"The sages. They say that the memory is the first thing to go." Aubrey patted his chest. "But don't worry, old man, they have drugs to slow the progression of dementia."

Chuckling at her ability to read him, he settled her on the couch. Thunder rumbled in the distance, and the wind blew the screen door shut with a slam, startling her.

She looked worried. "I hope it's just a passing storm. I *need* to finish that painting tomorrow."

Aubrey sounded downright desperate. Did she sense that the end was closer than he'd suspected?

Franco flicked on a couple lights. "I hope so too." Because how awful would it be if the cops hauled him off in handcuffs before she had a chance to realize her dream?

While he put on a pot of soup for her and made himself a sandwich, she talked about the painting, about others she'd left in the basement of her house... a house now owned by a couple from Detroit.

"What happened to your place?" he asked, ladling broth into a bowl.

"Sold it to cover my expenses. You'd be surprised how much isn't covered by insurance."

"You're preaching to the choir," he said. "I'm still digging out from under the bills that piled up after the accident. But I'm sure the buyers will return your things. Especially if you sic Agnes on 'em."

"No. I don't want them. You know how Picasso and Van Gogh had blue periods?"

Franco didn't, but he said, "Yeah..."

"Well, that stuff represents my morbid period. If the new owners are smart, they'll leave them right where they are, save themselves a lot of money in bug spray and mouse-traps."

The past few days, she'd grown more critical of herself. He let the crack about her artwork pass, thinking that when the time was right, he'd recite his list of her many admirable traits and talents.

He'd seen a couple of TV trays leaning against the back wall of the closet, and put one near the couch. When he placed a spoon and napkin on it, she said, "I'm not hungry."

"That's funny," he said, delivering the broth, "I don't recall asking if you were."

She started to protest.

"Use this for the soup," he said, handing her a straw. "It'll save all that up-and-down elbow motion." Then, grabbing the remote, he turned on the noon news. "Go on. Drink up. It's important for you to stay hydrated."

When the radar image of North Georgia lit the screen with bright yellow and green, she groaned. "That doesn't look promising, does it?"

No, it didn't. But she already looked depressed enough. "That's beautiful," he said, his gaze traveling to the right half of the canvas, where cumulus clouds and the shaggy trunks of oaks and sugar maples were reflected in the lake's mirror-like surface. "Hard to believe you got so much done in just a few hours."

She pointed out mistakes—too much yellow, not enough red, wrong shade of blue on the clouds' undersides, not quite the right light in Dusty's eyes, far too little joy in his smile. "God willing, I'll have time to address all of that tomorrow."

Fat raindrops pelted the windows as howling gusts buffeted the RV. If this kept up, she'd have no choice but to paint inside tomorrow. "Worst-case scenario," he said, pointing at the bright red catamaran she'd placed in the lower left-hand corner of the painting, "couldn't you use your imagination to finish, the way you did when you put Dusty into the canoe?"

"I'll do whatever it takes. If that means faking it a little, so be it." She paused, inspected her hands. "Of course, it won't be as precise and realistic as it might be, if I could paint what I see, outside, but..."

Eyes on the TV screen, Franco watched as the weatherman's forefinger followed the jet stream. "As you can see," he said, "a low pressure system has moved into the region, and its clockwise rotation could cause potentially heavy thunderstorms."

"Oh, great," Aubrey complained. "Can't we watch something other than this depressing forecast?"

Franco slid a disk into the DVD player, hit play, and she napped—a good long one—as Bob Ross worked in the background.

Shortly after supper, he popped the disk in again, and this time, Aubrey watched. She leaned back and put up her feet. "That mountain scene reminds me of the time my folks took me on a camping trip. In a six-man tent. With both sets of grandparents." Laughing, she said, "I thought Mama would pull out all her hair before the week ended."

He could picture Agnes, swatting mosquitoes and wrinkling her nose at the idea of doing her business in an outhouse.

"She surprised us all, figuring out ways to cook the craziest meals over a campfire—pizza, pot roast, even a pineapple upside-down cake—and for a while there, it even looked like she was enjoying herself."

"What happened? Did a bear wander through the campsite and fight her for the title of Grizzly Adams?"

Aubrey laughed, but it lacked the music he'd grown accustomed to hearing.

"You know as well as I do there aren't any grizzlies this far east. But there *are* black bears. And when Mama put the binoculars to her face and got an eyeful of a mother and her cubs..." Aubrey laughed again. "She wanted to pack up and go home. 'Who do you think I am, Little Red Riding Hood?'!"

It was good hearing that, despite Agnes, she'd had happy childhood memories.

"Dad razzed her about that trip every year for as long as I could remember."

"Did she get along well with your husband?"

"Get along well!" Aubrey shook her head. "Mama introduced us, nagged me relentlessly until I finally agreed to a date with him." She sighed. "Michael's parents were in Europe, or I might have played the 'They think I'm not rich enough for their boy' card. By the time they came back, we were already married."

What kind of people missed their son's wedding? *The type who raised a guy who left his wife when she needed him most,* Franco decided.

"It wasn't until I got sick and Michael left that Mama admitted she'd made a mistake. And you know? That was probably the only time she ever told me she was sorry, and I actually believed it." Aubrey smiled a little at the memory. "But it wasn't entirely her fault. I confused Michael's charm for decency, too… at first."

"Where is he now?"

"Oh, he's still in Savannah, living in the condo he owned before the wedding. He's in the import-export business—perfect for a nose-in-the-air guy like him." A harrumph, and then, "He gets to flaunt his so-called expertise on every subject under the sun, every chance he gets." Grinning, she concluded with, "You know what the biggest regret of his life is?"

"Losing you."

A rowdy laugh, and then, "Hardly! He had aspirations of becoming a Jeopardy contestant. He loved sitting in his leather recliner, shouting out the answers before the contestants did. And to give him his due, he was right about half the time."

"I hate that show. Makes me feel dumber than a box of rocks."

"Oh, don't be so hard on yourself. I'll bet you know lots of the answers, but like me, you just need a *smidge* more time to blurt 'em out."

"Yeah, but still."

"See, that's another way you and Michael are different. He didn't mind getting half the answers wrong, because he answered correctly more often than *I* did."

"Sheesh. He sounds like a real prince."

"Yeah, but as he was so fond of saying, 'It is what it is.'"

"I know the type: an arrogant gasbag."

"Couldn't have said it better myself." A sad little smile turned up the corners of her mouth. "You know, if my mom would just give you half a chance, I think she'd love you almost as much as I do."

Chapter Twenty-Four

LOVE? SHE WAS TALKING OUT OF HER HEAD, HE thought, putting away the supper dishes, but that was to be expected from someone with a brain tumor, right?

"You've known me, what, a month? Easy to play the good guy in such a short time, when there's nothing at stake."

"Evidently, you're forgetting how I treated you when we first met. I detested you, for no reason other than you pee standing up."

That took him by surprise. "I don't think I'll ever get used to your penchant for telling it like it is."

"Oh, in time you would have come to love me, too. But as I said, time is the one thing I don't have."

"Aubrey…"

"As for having nothing at stake, may I point out that you'll go to jail if the police catch up with us?"

Not *if*, he thought, but *when*.

"You risked everything to bring me here. That's the stuff heroes are made of."

Franco didn't see himself that way. Not even close. But her voice, her posture, her sunken eyes told him she'd had enough talk for one day.

He got to his feet, crossed the space between them in two strides. "It's past ten. Time for bed, missy."

He prepared himself for an argument, but Aubrey only sighed.

"Need help getting back there?"

She nodded, and he lifted her in one easy move. If he had to guess, Franco would say she'd lost ten, maybe twenty pounds since they'd met, and she hadn't exactly been a heavyweight on that first day. Aubrey was literally wasting away before his eyes. How much longer could she hold on at this rate?

Franco sat her on the foot of the bed and, without a word, slowly undressed her… and she let him. Her husband should be here doing things like this—helping her, supporting her, comforting her—not a near stranger. What kind of low-down skunk would turn his back on the woman he'd pledged to love and honor, in sickness and in health? *Michael,* he thought, teeth clenched, *you're riding a rocket straight to hell when* you *die.*

He'd barely finished tugging her sweatshirt down around her hips when she said, "I hate to be a pain, but I need to use the bathroom."

"You're not a pain," he ground out. And picking her up again, he added, "You're the toughest, strongest person I've ever met."

And there it was again, that sad little smile. "Franco Allessi, are you… are you *crying*?"

"'Course not," he said, settling her onto the toilet. "Got some lint in my eyes, thanks to that fleecy sweatshirt of yours."

"Something like *tears*?" She waved him away. "Can a girl get a little privacy?"

"Sure, sure, of course." He closed the door behind him. "But I'll be right here if you need me."

Forehead pressed to the cool faux wood, Franco held his breath. *Stop it. Just knock it off. Toughen up! She needs you to hold it together!*

A horrible thought struck him: *If it hurt this much now, how much worse would it be when she was gone?* It wasn't the same ache that he'd felt when the doctors told him that Jill wasn't going to make it. He'd spent twenty years loving the woman, being loved by her. In the short time since he'd met Aubrey, she'd often reminded him of Jill. Her toughness. Her big heart. Her stubbornness. Her ability to tell it like it is, all while making excuses for the bad behavior of others.

He heard the flush of the toilet. Running water. One hand on the doorknob, he waited, expecting her to tell him she was ready to get back to bed. What he heard instead nearly put him on his knees.

Aubrey, softly weeping.

She hovered on the threshold between life and death. It seemed to him that despite her gloomy jokes and well-rehearsed "So I'm dying, big deal" act, she was terrified. Who wouldn't be?

Franco went back into the bedroom and sat where she'd been moments ago, held his head in his hands, and sobbed. For Aubrey. For Jill and Tony. For Dusty and other patients, clinging to life at Savannah Falls, at hospice centers all over the world. And for himself. Because if he was half the man Aubrey had described, he'd know whether or not to go in there and hold her, or give her the privacy to grieve for her own life.

His wristwatch ticked, loud and steady, as if counting out the final beats of her heart. He took a deep breath and moved woodenly toward the bathroom door. "Hey," he said, knocking softly, "you didn't fall in, did you?"

"No." She blew her nose, and he heard the water running again. "I'm fine."

Aubrey was drying her hands when he opened the door. "From what I heard, *you* aren't."

He'd been careful not to make a sound, so how had she known that—

"You need new material. That 'you fell in' joke is as old as the hills and twice as dusty."

"Oh, like *that* line is brand-new." Franco's arm slid around her as if he'd been doing it all his life, and guided her back to the bed.

She climbed in and let him adjust the covers.

"Need anything before I go?"

"No. I'm fine." She held out her hand, and when he put his into it, she said, "Your wife was a lucky woman."

No, he thought, *she wasn't.* He'd been a self-centered jerk for most of his married life. "I was the lucky one," he admitted.

Eyes closed, she muttered, "Sez you." And just like that, Aubrey slept.

Back in the living room, he turned out the lights and muted the TV. It was a different experience, watching Bob Ross work minus the soothing voice. In this episode, the artist painted a moonlit, snow-capped mountain. Aubrey had never experienced a true autumn. Was the same true for a snowy winter? *Definitely something to ask her in the morning*, he thought, closing his eyes.

"Franco?"

He opened one eye and saw the DVD menu on the screen. A glance at his watch told him he'd been asleep more than an hour.

"Franco…"

He hustled down the hall and stood beside her. "What's up, kiddo? Thirsty? Need a pain pill?"

"No, no, I'm… I'm so cold."

She was only using half the bed, so he doubled the blanket and bedspread over her.

"Better?"

When she shook her head, he raced back down the hall to gather up his linens. But even with the extra quilt, Aubrey continued shivering.

"I could pile bath towels and jackets on top of that… or get into bed beside you, let my body heat warm you up."

She patted the mattress, then rolled onto her side. "Would you? Please?"

Franco slid under the covers and tucked in close behind her. It took a full five minutes before her breathing slowed and she stopped shaking—he knew exactly how long it had taken, because he'd watched every flick of the glowing blue numbers on the LED alarm on the night table.

Being this close to her was the oddest sensation, because not once in their hours together had she roused sexual feelings in him. She still hadn't. And yet, he'd never felt this way about any woman, not even Jill. Franco held her a little tighter. With time running out, this was as close as they'd ever be. If only he could share good health and stamina the way he was sharing warmth.

Aubrey moved, and he whispered, "Sorry. Didn't mean to wake you."

"I'm the most selfish woman on earth."

"That's crazy talk."

"You realize how much trouble you're in?" was her sleepy reply.

"Trouble?"

"If the cops find us, you might have to serve time. And not just fifty hours of community service."

Yeah, he knew, and didn't care. It felt good, felt *right*, doing these small things for her. The ugly truth was, when he got out of jail—however long that might take—he'd still be alive. And

Aubrey? Aubrey would be—

"I'm positively evil, asking you to take such a risk."

"You didn't hold a gun to my head. I'm a big boy. Could have said no, if I'd wanted to."

"I know."

She was quiet long enough that he thought she'd fallen asleep.

"Have I told you lately how much I appreciate what you're doing?"

"Shh. Get some sleep."

More silence, and then, "Franco… listen."

"To what?"

"Has it stopped raining?"

"How would I know," he said, kissing the back of her head, "with you talking nonstop?"

She snickered. "Okay. I can take a hint."

"Uh-huh. Right."

"You know what I wonder?"

"No, but I'd bet my suspended driver's license that you're about to tell me."

"I wonder what I ever did in my life to deserve a friend like you."

"Funny. I wonder the same thing."

She folded her arms atop his. "I meant what I said out there earlier, you know."

"No, I don't know. You said, like, ten thousand words. Ten million, even."

"I said I love you. And I do. Not like *guy-girl* love or anything. More like a dad."

"Sheesh. I'm nowhere near old enough to be your father!"

"A brother, then."

"I've never been a big brother, but I had the best example of one. Yeah, I think I can live with that."

"You would have been a great dad."

He felt her take a deep breath, let it out slowly.

"Why didn't you and Jill ever have kids?"

"Let's just say I was an immature, self-absorbed idiot, and let it go at that, okay?"

"Franco Allessi, why oh why are you so tough on yourself? Jill fell in love with you for a reason." She squeezed his arms again. "Tell me. Tell me why she married you."

"She was pregnant." After all these years, why did it still hurt so much to say that?

Aubrey rolled onto her back. "Miscarriage?"

He rolled onto his back too. "Stillbirth."

On her other side now, she faced him. "Oh, Franco. How awful. For both of you."

He tucked both hands under his head. "It was a long, long time ago."

"Let me guess: that's when you started drinking?"

"No, that's when *Jill* started drinking. Took her years, but she finally beat it." He looked over at her. "You remind me a lot of her. She was resilient, stubborn, strong…"

Aubrey cleared her throat. "So *your* problem, it started after—"

"After she died. Yeah. Jill was the glue that held us together. She did it all. And when I lost her, well, I guess I lost my way… lost myself for a while."

She put her head on his shoulder. "You're pretty strong and resilient, too, y'know."

For now, that's how it might appear. But how long could he continue the pretense?

"So why didn't you and *Michael* have any kids?"

"I would have sworn I told you." Aubrey shrugged. "Damn brain tumor. I hate being forgetful and sounding stupid."

"You aren't forgetful and—"

She pressed a finger to his lips. "Yes, I am. Now what was I saying? Oh, that's right. Children. We didn't have any," she said, echoing Franco's scorn, "because, well, because Michael was *Michael*."

For a long while, the only sound in the room was the drumming of rain on the roof and her soft, steady breaths. His arm was going to sleep, but Franco ignored it. He liked taking care of someone—of *Aubrey*—for a change. If by some miracle she survived this death sentence, he'd keep right on taking care of her. Grinning, he remembered her *not guy-girl love* wisecrack. First chance he got, he'd tell her that he felt the same way.

And that he'd miss her like crazy, for the rest of his life.

Chapter Twenty-Five

"IT'S A MIRACLE," SHE SAID WHEN HE ROLLED HER nearer the water.

"A *rainbow*." Aubrey looked up at him. "Franco... a rainbow!"

It didn't take long for her to get set up and start adding it to the painting.

"What do you think? Does it look genuine?"

"It does. It's gorgeous. But then you knew that. You're good at what you do. Real good. There isn't a thing wrong with admitting it."

When she smiled, Franco noticed that a pink flush had colored her cheeks. Happiness? Contentment? Then he noticed a peculiar sheen in her blue eyes. Fever? *Only one way to find out*, he thought, pressing his lips to her forehead.

"What was that for?" she asked, grinning up at him.

"You're feverish. My mom never relied on a thermometer. She said this was the only way to know for sure." He kissed her forehead again. "You have a fever."

"I know." She went back to work on Dusty's face. "But so what? It isn't like some little temperature spike is gonna kill me."

He raised his arms, let them fall against his sides. "You're impossible. I say we should think about getting back to the hospice."

"Absolutely not. I'm close..." She tapped the canvas with the hard end of her paintbrush. "Real close. I can't quit now."

"*How* close? An hour? Three?"

"I don't know. It'll be done when it's done." She grinned, barely. "Park it, Allessi, and stop rushing me."

He straddled the stool, but everything in him said they should pack up and leave. Get her to a hospital, ASAP, where they'd put her on IVs—pain meds, fluids, whatever it took to make her last hours a little easier, a little more comfortable.

"What do you think? Did I capture Dusty's character or what!"

Franco barely glanced at the painting. Being here hadn't seemed wrong before she'd developed the fever. But now? Now he couldn't concentrate on anything except what it meant: she was down to the last few grains of sand in the hourglass; if he couldn't convince her to do the right thing, she'd die a painful, miserable death, and it would be his fault.

"You know that other painting in my pack?"

"The one of your folks? Yeah, I saw it. Why?"

"I want you to give it to my mom. This one, of course, goes to Dusty's folks. Everything else, the kit, the sketches, the stuff in my room at Savannah Falls, I want you to have—"

The wail of sirens interrupted her. They were close. Real close. And Franco knew whom they were for.

It happened fast.

Tires, spewing gravel as squad cars came to a grinding halt.

The slam of car doors.

Cops, guns drawn, surrounded them.

"Franco Allessi?"

"Yeah…"

"Hands up!" one officer bellowed.

Another shouted, "On your knees!"

He did as he was told as a third read him his rights and a fourth cuffed him.

Aubrey was on her feet, staggering, wide-eyed and crying. "Let him go! You don't understand!"

"He's wanted for kidnapping," the first cop said, "for starters."

"But… but this was all *my* idea. He's only here as a favor to *me*."

A sheen of perspiration coated her flushed face.

"You know she's dying, right?" Franco growled. "Did her mother tell you *that*? She has a fever, and she's lightheaded. You jerks need to call an ambulance, get her to the nearest hospital. I won't give you any trouble. But do the right thing, okay guys? Take care of her before you haul me away."

As if on cue, a rescue van lurched to a stop and three EMTs rushed forward. Two caught her before she went down, and the driver rolled a gurney closer. In one blink, they strapped her in. In the next, they moved her to the waiting ambulance.

She grabbed the nearest paramedic's sleeve. "Please, *please,* at least let me talk to him!"

"She doesn't look too good," said his partner. "What could it hurt?"

The cops brought Franco to his feet and walked him over.

"I'm sorry," Aubrey told him. "So, so very sorry." She glanced around, at the EMTs, at the cops, at the crowd of curious campers that had gathered. "I did this to you. And now? Now they're going to take you away and I'll never have a chance to make it up to you."

She was sobbing as he said, "You listen to me, Aubrey Brewer, and you listen good! You have nothing to be sorry for. Nothing, you hear? Everything's gonna be okay." He forced a smile. "I'll be fine, and so will you. Soon as I get this straightened out, I'll come see you. So you hold on, okay?"

She bit her lower lip, looked toward the easel and the painting that, except for her signature, was finished.

Franco nodded toward her things. "You guys mind grabbing her stuff? That painting is a gift. It's the reason she wanted to come here, to paint it for the kid who has the room next to hers at the hospice center."

"What can it hurt," the cop repeated, and started packing things up.

"Get her out of here," Franco said. "She has glioblastoma multiforme. Brain tumor. The worst kind. She needs her meds. Tell the hospital staff to call Savannah Falls. Talk to Mrs. Kane. She'll tell them everything they need to know."

The second cop scribbled everything Franco had said into his notebook.

"You came into my life at the perfect moment. If there's a heaven," she said, "I'll be up there, watching over you." She grabbed his sleeve. "When I get up there, I'll look for Jill. I'll tell her all about what you did for me. And then? And then I'll send you a sign, so you'll know we're both all right... the love of your life, and your best friend. I'll watch out for you..."

"Cut it out, Aubrey. You're not going anywhere just yet, except to the hospital," he said, his voice cracking. "You hang on until I can get things straightened out, you hear?" He felt selfish and self-centered, asking such a thing of her, because at this point, death would be a welcome reprieve from all she'd suffered. "You try to hang on until I get there. I mean it, okay?"

Her voice was small and weak when she quoted Yoda: "'Do or do not; there *is* no try.'"

And as the ambulance doors closed, he heard her say, "I love you, Franco Allessi. Always remember: you're a good and decent man."

He was crying hard when they put him into the back of a squad car.

Because he'd never see her again, and he knew it.

Chapter Twenty-Six

WHEN THE STATE POLICE CALLED TO SAY THEY'D FOUND Aubrey at the Moccasin Creek State Campground—and that she was alive— Agnes's knees nearly gave way. She slumped into the nearest chair.

"Thank God," she whispered. "Oh, thank God. Which hospital did they take her to?"

"Your daughter insisted on coming home, to Savannah," he said. "She refused the Medevac chopper... said it should remain available for, ah, someone else."

Knowing Aubrey, she'd said, "For someone who has a chance to *live*."

"She's on her way to Memorial University Medical Center," the officer said. "Unless they hit traffic, ETA is three hours."

If Aubrey lasted that long, it would be Agnes's last time with her daughter. A sob ached in her throat, but she bottled it up. There'd be plenty of time for tears later.

"Can we send a car to take you to the hospital, ma'am?"

"No..." When it was time to leave, she didn't want to be at the mercy of some poor trooper to fetch her and deliver her home again. "But thank you. You've been very kind."

"Got something handy to write with?"

She did not, but Agnes wanted to hang up. There were things to do. Plans to make. People to call. She rummaged through her purse and, using a tube of lipstick, wrote across her wallet as he rattled off his name and number.

"If you need anything, *anything*," he said, "just give me a call."

"Thank you."

"Any questions before I let you go?"

"Did you get that… that *criminal* who kidnapped her?"

"Mr. Allessi is in custody. But your daughter insisted the whole thing was her idea. Said if anybody was kidnapped, it was Mr. Allessi."

"Aubrey has a brain tumor. She's desperate and dying. And that vile man took advantage of her. I hope you didn't believe him. And I hope he rots in jail."

After a considerable pause, the trooper said, "Well, if you need anything, you know how to reach me."

"Thank you," she said again, and hung up. But he wouldn't hear from her, even if the information she'd written hadn't already smeared. What use did she have for a man so stupid as to believe Aubrey's ridiculous story?

Agnes made her way to the kitchen and put on a pot of coffee. Then, grabbing her address book, she sat near the phone so she could begin making calls. Staring at the to-do list she'd tucked under the F-for-Funeral tab, her eyes filled with tears: Item number one, "write obituary," had a line drawn through it, because Aubrey had written it months ago, on the very afternoon Dr. Oken delivered the terminal diagnosis. The envelope read FOR INSERTION IN THE SAVANNAH TRIBUNE. THANKS, MAMA, LOVE, AUBREY. Agnes had promised not to open it until, as Aubrey had put it, "it was time."

The coffeepot hissed, its signal that the last drops of water had percolated through the filter. She poured a cup of the strong black brew, returned to the table, opened the envelope, and read:

My name is Aubrey Agnes Anderson Brewer, Savannah native and only child of Aaron and Agnes Anderson. If you're reading this, you already know that I'm dead. (Sorry. I know that was tough to read, but trust me, it was tough to write, too.)

Dying doesn't make me special. People do it every minute of every day. Even people who fight it—and if you knew me, you're aware that I fought it, hard. I fought in memory of my dad, who lived every day as if it were his last. For my mother, who took great pride in planning my every achievement. For my ex, Michael Brewer, who is only my ex because his oh-so-delicate heart couldn't bear to watch me suffer. For my students and fellow teachers at the Savannah School of the Arts. And I fought for myself, because let's face it, nobody wants to die.

But let's not get all maudlin over this, okay? Instead, I invite you to read Henry Van Dyke's poem, "Gone from My Sight," a message that is powerful and true: "Even as you say, 'There, she is gone,' those on the other side will yell 'Hooray! Here she comes!'

Oh, and that nagging voice you'll hear from the back of your mind? That'll be me, reminding you to hug the people who matter to you. Tell them you love them, now, while you can. And please, please don't cry because I'm gone; laugh because I was here!

Agnes plucked a napkin from the basket on the table and dried her eyes, then returned the obituary to its envelope and pressed it to her chest. She could almost hear Aubrey saying, "Quit crying, Mama. There's work to do, and time's a-wastin'."

She opened the address book, flipped to the D page and dialed her pastor. Yes, of course he'd officiate at the funeral, the pastor, and he promised to recite a graveside sermon as well. Next, she called the funeral home, put them on alert that she'd need a medium-sized room for the viewing, and declined their polite offer to write Aubrey's obituary. Agnes left messages all over town—the garden society, book club, ladies' auxiliary— and hoped she hadn't forgotten anyone who'd feel slighted by an unintended oversight.

If the trooper had been correct, Agnes had two hours or so to shower and change and get to the hospital. She wanted to be there when the ambulance arrived. Those last months before moving into Savannah Falls, Aubrey had stayed right here, in her old room. That would make it easy to pack a few things for her. A pretty nightgown. Slippers—though something told her they wouldn't be worn—a robe and rudimentary toiletries.

Weeks ago, Aubrey had told her which dress she wanted to wear during her final hours on earth.

"My going-away outfit," she'd said, describing the bright blue sundress.

"Spaghetti straps? But Aubrey, what if... what if it happens during the wintertime?"

Aubrey had given her a playful elbow jab. "Don't worry, Mama," she'd said, laughing. "I won't catch a chill. I'll be *dead*."

"Honestly, Aubrey. Sometimes I'm just at a loss with you."

"I know, I know. 'You inherited your father's height. His beautiful blue eyes. His intelligence,'" Aubrey quoted, "'but why oh why did you have to inherit his macabre sense of humor, too?'"

Agnes rooted through her daughter's closet, found the sundress, and hung it on the hook behind the door. She pressed its hem to her cheek, thinking it had been a good choice, because it would bring out the blue of Aubrey's eyes.

She headed for the shower, imagining what Aubrey would have said about that: "Nobody will notice if it matches or not, Mama, because my eyes will be *closed*."

***

When they brought Aubrey in, she was barely breathing, and yet she reached for Agnes's hand.

"Mama," she murmured. "I'm so glad you're here."

While the nurses got her situated in the ICU, Agnes made up her mind not to mention the disappearance or the horrible man who'd taken her away. It would only upset Aubrey, and she didn't want their last interaction to be strained or angry.

Now, attached to IV tubes and wires that signaled the monitors, Aubrey so looked small and frail, almost grey against the white sheets and pillowcase. Agnes pulled a chair close to the bed and grasped her daughter's cool, limp fingertips.

She'd seen a blanket warmer around the hall, and thanks to those last days with her husband, Agnes knew how to use it. Draping the warmed coverlet over Aubrey, she said, "There now. That's better, isn't it."

Aubrey's eyelids fluttered, then opened. "Where is he?"

"Who? Michael?" Agnes had made a dozen phone calls. How could she have forgotten to call her son-in-law of all people!

"No." Aubrey frowned. "Not Michael. Franco. He said... said he'd try to—"

"Bree," Agnes interrupted, "stop talking. Just rest, please?"

"You have to tell them. You have to tell them, Mama!"

She'd seen her daughter angry. Happy. Afraid. This mood was completely new, and Agnes had no idea how to interpret it.

"Promise me, Mama. Promise me you'll tell them."

"Who's *them*?"

"The police... tell them... tell them it was *my* idea to leave, not Franco's."

Agnes sat up straighter, turned Aubrey's hand loose. She couldn't do that. *Wouldn't* do that. The man had stolen her only child away, stolen her precious last hours with her daughter.

"You *know* me, Mama. You know it's true."

"Aubrey, please. I asked you to stop talk—"

"You have to tell them. It's the right thing to do."

Agnes remembered the conversation in Aubrey's room at Savannah Falls, mere days before she'd disappeared, and finally had a description for that unfamiliar expression: desperation. Aubrey had seemed frantic and determined to get to the mountains, so that she could see and paint the autumn leaves before she died.

And you said no.

"Fix it, Mama. He shouldn't be punished. Not for something I did. He was so good to me."

If you had said yes...

"He's a good man." Aubrey inhaled a ragged breath. "He knew what you'd do if he took me, but he took me anyway."

Eyes closed, Agnes fought tears. It was hard, so very hard, watching her only child in this condition, watching the sweet little girl who'd been a bundle of energy, the woman she'd become, who'd lived life to the fullest, struggling for every breath.

"Do it for me, Mama. I've always, *always* done what you asked. Musical instruments. Athletics. College. Career. Marriage. I did it all. I did it for *you.*"

But those were good choices, smart *choices,* Agnes thought, *things that were good for you, Aubrey!* She opened her eyes, and saw that Aubrey was crying. Hard. Spending precious energy, fighting on behalf of *that awful man*!

"Aubrey, I won't say it again. *Please. Be. Quiet.*"

"I will, just as soon as you promise..."

How could Aubrey ask such a thing of her, especially at a time like this!

"I said yes," Aubrey rasped. "Said yes to *everything* you asked of me, Mama." She inhaled another raspy breath. "I did it because I love you. Because I didn't want to disappoint you." "You know the truth," she'd said, seconds ago. Yes, Agnes admitted, Aubrey had done all those things. The truth? She'd *known* her daughter couldn't—wouldn't—say no to anything she asked of her.

"Do you love me, Mama?"

"What? Aubrey! What a question!"

"Answer me. I need to know. Have you *ever* loved me?"

"Of course I love you. From the moment they put you into my arms in the hospital, to this moment, I've loved you more than anything or anyone in the world."

"Then prove it."

"By… by telling the police to release that terrible man?"

"He isn't terrible. He's my dearest friend. The only person in years who gave a damn what *I* wanted. Who listened to me. Really listened. Who made my greatest dream come true. When you see the painting of Dusty, you'll understa—"

"You're on the verge of hysteria, Bree. Calm down, or I'll call the nurse. Ask her to give you something."

"Something that'll drug me into a stupor? So you won't have to listen? So you can control even my last breaths? Is that how you want to spend our final moments together?"

"What I want, Bree, is for you to be quiet and settle down."

"I'll do anything you ask… *if you promise.*"

"To tell them it was your idea. That this… this *Franco* person had nothing to do with it?"

Aubrey gave one weak nod of her head. "Yes."

"But Bree…"

"My name is *Aubrey*. I've never liked being called *Bree.* I told you and told you, but did you care? No! You want what you want, when you want it. I've never asked you for anything, Mama, but I'm asking you to promise you'll fix things so that Franco won't pay a price for what I did… for what you *know* I did."

The clock on the wall kept time with Aubrey's heartbeats being counted out by each *beep* of the monitor. If she made this pledge, would it guarantee Aubrey a few hours more—time enough to make sure she slipped quietly, peacefully into death, instead of struggling and straining, trying to draw a promise from her own mother?

Agnes admitted that Aubrey had been right. She'd spent countless hours and energy bending her daughter's will to meet her own. Every decision had been the end product of careful thought, because she'd only wanted the best for her only child. The result? A lifetime of basking in the glow of admiration, from members of her church, the garden club ladies, bridge partners, and sorority sisters. Every glimmer of joy that lit her life had emanated from Aubrey.

"All right, Aubrey. I promise. I'll talk to the police. To the judge. To anyone who will listen. I'll tell them he's completely innocent of the charges." She grabbed her daughter's hand. "Will that make you happy?"

A look of serenity replaced pained desperation on Aubrey's face. Her breathing returned to normal, and the beeps of the heart monitor slowed.

"Good." She smiled. Gave Agnes's hand a slight squeeze. "I'm trusting you to do it, putting all my faith in you. Please don't let me down, Mama."

Chapter Twenty-Seven

A SANE, RATIONAL MAN WOULD BE SCARED OUT OF HIS socks. They'd probably throw the book at him, but strangely, Franco wasn't afraid. Rather, he was glad he'd helped Aubrey realize her dream, and if he had it to do over, he would, in exactly the same way. For the first time since Jill's death, he believed in himself, felt like the man depicted in Aubrey's watercolor painting. No matter what they did to him, he'd always have that.

Carlisle showed up and, just as he had that morning so many weeks ago, stood on the other side of the holding cell and said, "The county has sent me to represent you. There are a few loose ends to tie up before we go before Judge Malloy, but—"

"How's Aubrey? Have you heard anything? Where did they take her?"

"I'll see what I can find out. Meanwhile, though, you need to bring me up to speed. Tell me everything. Start at the beginning." He sat on the bench against the wall, blue-lined yellow tablet on his knees and pen at the ready.

"She's gone, Franco."

Both men looked up, into the haggard face of Agnes Anderson.

Franco gripped the bars so tightly, his fingers ached. "When?"

"About three hours ago."

"Aw, damn. *Damn.*" Tears stung his eyes. "Was it... did she go easy?"

"Yes. We had a long talk. It was a good talk. Then she fell asleep, and that was… and that was it. She went very peacefully."

Forehead pressed to his fists, he whispered, "Well, thank God for that."

"You can thank God for much *more* than that," Agnes said, stepping up close. "She made me promise—almost with her last breath—to make sure the proper people are made aware that leaving Savannah Falls was her idea. That she planned the whole thing, all on her own, with no input from you."

A sob ached in his throat, but he didn't dare give in to it. Not here. Not now. Not in front of Agnes, who would no doubt delight in seeing him lose control.

"You're willing to testify to that?" Carlisle asked her.

Agnes lifted her chin. "I am. It's what Aubrey would have wanted."

She aimed that steely gaze Franco's way to add, "She called you her best friend. Said you'd done things no one else could— or would—and that you made her last days the happiest, most fulfilling of her life."

"And I… I feel the same way." He inhaled a big, shaky breath. "She was some woman, that daughter of yours."

"You were in love with her?" Carlisle asked. "I could use that when presenting the case to Malloy. Love makes people do some crazy things."

"It wasn't like that between us." He looked at Agnes. "I hope you'll believe that, Mrs. Anderson." Franco paused, collecting his thoughts, gathering self-control. "Aubrey was like a younger sister and a best friend, all rolled into one. I respected her. Admired her. And yes, I loved her. I'll *always* love her. But I wasn't *in love* with her."

"That's too bad. 'Cause like I said, love makes people do crazy things." Carlisle buckled up his briefcase and signaled the guard. "I'll be back in a few hours, hopefully with your release papers." On the threshold of the big metal door leading to the cells, he added, "I'll do my best, but don't hold your breath."

The guard hesitated. "You coming, too, ma'am?"

"Yes." She faced the exit, then turned to Franco again. "Thank you, Mr. Allessi... Franco, for being the friend my daughter needed."

As the hours passed, Franco relived those final days with Aubrey. The tears he expected never materialized. Maybe later, maybe not. Part of him was happy for her. No more pain. No more suffering. He'd be one selfish s.o.b. to hold on-to her, knowing she could finally be free of all that.

A guard came in, asked if he needed to use the men's room before being escorted to the courtroom. He did. Stopped at the water fountain for a quick sip, too.

"Shame about your friend," the man said.

"Yeah, but she's in a better place."

"Yeah," the guard echoed, shoving through the court-room door, "we can hope."

Carlisle, seated at the table facing the judge's bench, mo-tioned to him. "I emailed a pleading to Malloy, explaining what happened." He crossed his fingers. "Maybe he's in a good mood for a change."

Franco quoted the guard. "We can hope."

Malloy entered with a flourish, starting the proceedings with a bang of his gavel.

"Mr. Allessi," he said, one bushy brow high on his fore-head. "I have to admit, I didn't expect to see you again. Espe-cially not so soon."

Not knowing how to respond, Franco said nothing.

"What do you have to say for yourself, sir?"

Between the arrest and now, he'd had hours to rehearse his speech. But Franco's mind went blank.

"No point wasting your time, Your Honor, so I'll just say I helped out a friend." He stood a little taller, lifted his chin. "And I have no regrets."

Malloy sat back, hands folded on his ponderous belly, nodding thoughtfully. "I've read Mr. Carlisle's summation, and I must say, this is a first. I've decided to let you go. The bailiff will show you where to sign, and he'll return your driver's license. I'll leave it up to you to decide whether or not you will complete your fifty hours at Savannah Falls. As far as I'm concerned, you've served your sentence."

"Thank you, Your Honor."

"You're quite welcome, Mr. Allessi. And may I say that I'm thoroughly impressed. I can count on one hand the number of times I've said that to anyone and have fingers left over." He banged his gavel and thundered "Next case!"

Carlisle grabbed Franco's elbow and led him from the courtroom.

"Man. You lucked out today, dude."

Franco remembered one of the last things Aubrey had told him: if there was a heaven, she'd watch over him.

"Luck had nothing to do with it," he said, "*dude.*"

Chapter Twenty-Eight

IT HAD TAKEN A FEW PHONE CALLS TO FIND OUT WHICH funeral home and cemetery Agnes had chosen. The funeral guy said Agnes only wanted one viewing, and Franco decided against showing up there. Wouldn't attend the funeral service, either. Instead, he'd go to the cemetery for his final goodbye.

The days until Aubrey's funeral passed slowly, despite completing his final hours at the hospice. Dusty's mom cried when she saw the painting, and said it was all the more precious because Aubrey hadn't put on the final touch, her signature.

He killed a little more time cleaning his trailer. Catching up on laundry. Washing the Jeep and weeding the pathetic excuse for a flower bed that ran alongside his front walk. When he finished, the place would have passed muster with even the most demanding drill sergeant. Again.

He signed up for classes at the college, too, just as he'd told Aubrey he would, then drove into town to buy a suit. The salesman tried to talk him into black, but Franco knew how she would have reacted to that, and he chose a gray pinstripe, instead. On the way home, he stopped at the barbershop for a shave and a haircut, found a big-box store and bought some shoe polish.

Now, he stood ten yards or so from the last row of the mourners that huddled under a big green awning. *Aubrey would have loved this sunny, blustery weather,* he thought, leaning one shoulder against a tree trunk. She would have loved listening as, one by one, students, coworkers, and friends delivered "I remember Aubrey" speeches. She would have liked Dusty's words most of all, because the kid had captured not only their relationship, but her personality with just a few, well-chosen words: "She was a friend, even when I didn't think I wanted one. Because she got me. Aubrey really *got* me."

Franco scanned the crowd, looking for her ex-husband. He'd bet everything he owned that Michael was the paunchy, bespectacled, balding-and-bearded guy to Agnes's right, mopping his eyes with a big white hanky. He was every bit the foppish scene-stealer Aubrey had described, and Franco could only shake his head. "Where were you when she needed you, ya big phony," he muttered. "Sure as hell not front and center!"

The preacher took his place at the head of the flower-cloaked casket and, Bible open on his right palm, said, "I'm not going to keep you long. It's chilly out, and Aubrey wouldn't approve of me making you suffer through yet another sermon."

Soft laughter rippled through the crowd, and when it waned, he continued. "Some of you may know that this was Aubrey's favorite verse—and the only one she could recite by heart. It's First Corinthians, chapter ten, verse thirteen." He cleared his throat and read, "'No temptation has overtaken you except what is common to mankind. And God is faithful; he will not let you be tempted beyond what you can bear. But when you are tempted, he will also provide a way out so you can endure it.'"

What Franco knew about scripture would fit in a thimble. Funny, but Aubrey had never mentioned Bible verses, and they'd never discussed faith—or the lack of it—in any meaningful way. But it didn't surprise him to hear that this had been her favorite verse, or that she'd drawn enough comfort from it to memorize it. She'd toughed out the cancer like a real trouper. *"If there's a heaven…"* Something told him she believed there was. For her sake, Franco hoped so. Because if anyone deserved to spend eternity in paradise, it was Aubrey Brewer.

Quiet fluttering drew his attention upward, to the branches of the maple tree. It was Aubrey's blue jay. He knew, because of its unique crest. It had to be at least three miles between the cemetery and Savannah Falls. The jay hopped to another branch, one closer to Franco, and tilted its head. "Well, I'll be," he said.

It flew off, perched for an instant on a push-handle of Dusty's wheelchair, then darted under the awning and swooped low, almost colliding with Michael's head. The man ducked, crying out like a terrified little girl as the bird landed on the coffin, where it pecked gently at one of the roses that blanketed the gleaming, burled mahogany. A strange sound issued from it—not the *putt-putt* or squawk so typical of jays—but a pitiful, plaintive cry. Soft gasps drifted through the shady space, telling Franco that he wasn't the only one Aubrey had told about her relationship with the bird.

It returned to the branch above Franco's head. "How did you find her?" he asked.

The jay hopped left, cocked its head, and emitted a soft *putt-putt* sound.

"If I didn't know better," he whispered, "I'd say Aubrey sent you here."

The bird repeated its sad call, then flew to the top of the tree and out of sight.

The quiet rustle of people making their way to the parking lot brought his attention back to the awning. Agnes had hung back, and pressed a palm to the sleek casket lid. She wasn't crying, but puffy, red-rimmed eyes told him she had been. The preacher led her to a waiting car, and just before she climbed into the back seat, Agnes looked up, locking eyes with Franco. Something—not anger, not grief—called out to him. He committed the look to his memory. He'd likely never see Aubrey's stern, stiff-backed mother again, but they'd always have two things in common.

They'd both loved her.

And they'd both miss her, always.

Chapter Twenty-Nine

AUBREY HAD BEEN GONE NEARLY A MONTH, AND FRANCO wanted a drink. Couldn't remember wanting one more. There was beer in the fridge and wine in the cupboard, and an unopened fifth of whiskey under the sink. He licked his lips. Salivated. Got up from the couch and crossed to the kitchen...

... and dumped every bit of booze down the sink, can by can, bottle by bottle.

He still hadn't called his parents, and he'd promised Aubrey that he would. Franco knew the number by heart, even though he hadn't dialed it in ages.

"Hey, Mama," he said when she answered.

"Franco!"

He heard a click, and knew that his dad had picked up the extension.

"How goes it, son?"

"It goes." He smiled. It was good, really good, to hear their voices. "So I was wondering... what are you guys doing next week?"

"We're retired, so same as always: nothing," his dad joked.

"I have two weeks. Thought I'd drive up, spend 'em at home."

"Just in time for Thanksgiving," his dad said.

"We'll have dinner at the house this year," his mom put in, "instead of a restaurant. I'll invite the whole family!"

They sounded happy, and remembering that line from Aubrey's obituary, it made him feel good: "Hug the people who matter to you. Tell them you love them, now, while you can."

"Love you guys," he said, and after he hung up, Franco called Mrs. Kane.

"Did I miss something?" she asked. "I thought you rounded out your fifty hours weeks ago."

"I did. But I want to come back. As a volunteer. I thought I'd give you a heads-up, so you can figure out how I can help." He told her his schedule at the garage. Said that he'd be in New Hampshire for two weeks, visiting his folks, and that he'd signed up for classes at the community college, and planned to start a landscaping company just as soon as he'd saved up enough to buy some equipment. "But I'm free most weekends."

"We'll be thrilled to have you," she said.

He hung up, feeling more like the man Aubrey described than ever before. Franco didn't quite believe her words just yet, and knew that he might never live up to her image of him. But it was a good goal to shoot for. Something that would keep him on the straight and narrow, especially knowing she was up there, watching over him.

A knock at the door interrupted his musing. Who could that be at ten on a Saturday morning?

"Agnes?"

"I'm surprised, too," she said.

Franco stepped back, waving her inside. "Come in out of the cold. Make yourself comfortable."

She carried two big tote bags, each filled to the brim.

"What's all this?" he asked, relieving her of them.

"Things Aubrey wanted you to have." She shrugged out of her coat, and as Franco hung it on the hall tree, she added, "I should have come sooner. But—"

"Say no more," he interrupted. "You've had a lot on your plate. Can I get you a soda? Iced tea? Bottled water?"

"Coffee would be great, but don't go to the bother of brewing a new pot just for me."

"It's no bother." He filled the carafe and put grounds into the basket, then led her to the living room and invited her to sit as he went through the bags.

"This is unexpected," he admitted.

"She said you'd say that."

First thing to appear: a framed photo of Aubrey with her students, taken on the day of the fake birthday party. He smiled. "That threw her for a loop, didn't it."

"It did."

"Wait," he said, withdrawing her paint kit. So Aubrey had meant it when she said he should have it? "She didn't mean for me to have *this*. You want it, right?"

"Aubrey didn't inherit her artistic talents from me, so it would only gather dust at my place." She smiled. "But she said you showed some interest in painting."

"I've never tried." But he would now, just to see if Aubrey's prediction had been on target.

By the time both bags were emptied—of the Bob Ross book he'd given her, of her collection of the artist's DVDs— the coffeepot stopped gurgling. "Milk and sugar?"

"Just black, thanks."

He returned with two mugs, and once he sat down, Agnes handed him an envelope.

Franco opened it, and withdrew a postcard-sized painting of a sunrise. "Grief never ends," it read, "but it changes. It's a passage, not a place to stay. Grief is not a sign of weakness, nor a lack of faith. Grief is the price of love."

"She gave me one just like it," Agnes said. "I framed it and put it on my mantel."

He got up, crossed to his fake fireplace, and leaned it against the wall, directly under the painting she'd done of him. When he returned to the recliner, she produced a bottle of wine from her enormous purse.

205

"I thought we could toast Aubrey," she said.

"I'm happy to pour you a glass, but I can't join you. See, I'm a recovering alcoholic."

"Oh." She slid the bottle back into her purse. "Coffee is fine, then."

She lifted her mug, and he clinked his against it.

"I have a cheeseball and crackers, if you're hungry."

"Sounds delicious. May I help?"

In the kitchen, he handed her a box of crackers and a saucer, plopped the cheese ball into a bowl and grabbed a butter knife. "Sorry," he said, carrying it to the coffee table. "I don't entertain much, so I don't have the proper serving utensils."

"It wouldn't taste any different if you did." "*That* sounds like something Aubrey might say." Agnes smiled at that.

Franco picked up the DVD collection. "Say, how would you feel about watching one of these with me?"

"Now?"

"Unless you have somewhere else to be…"

"I'm almost ashamed to admit it, but I've never seen the man's work."

"You're in for a real treat, then." Franco popped in the disk and settled onto the loveseat beside her.

When the first video ended, she refilled their mugs. "Would you mind if I stayed and watched another one with you?"

"I'd like that."

They talked quietly as Bob created a mountain here, a babbling brook there. Their synchronized "And a happy little tree lives right here" prompted laughter, a blessed relief from the strain and pain of their shared loss. It seemed the most natural thing in the world to slide an arm over her shoulders. If he'd known it would make her cry, Franco would have kept his distance. But it didn't take long to realize she needed a hug, needed comfort, every bit as much—probably even more— than he did.

"How like Aubrey," she said when her tears subsided, "to leave us with the one thing we need most."

"Friendship," they said together.

"And she did it," Franco pointed out, "in just fifty hours."

About the Author

Best-selling author Loree Lough once sang for her supper, performing across the US and Canada. Now and then she blows the dust off her six-string to croon a tune or two, but mostly she writes novels that have earned hundreds of industry and "Readers' Choice" awards, four- and five-star reviews, and five book-to-movie options. At last count, Loree had 115 award-winning books on the shelves (nearly 7,000,000 copies in print).

Loree enjoys sharing learned-the-hard-way lessons about the craft and the industry, and her comedic how-to approach makes her a favorite speaker at writers' organizations, book clubs, private and government institutions, and college and high school writing programs in the US and abroad. She and her husband live near Baltimore and spend as much time as possible at their cabin in the Allegheny Mountains, where Loree continues to hone her "identify the critter tracks" skills.

A writer who believes in giving back, Loree dedicates a generous portion of her income to favorite charities. (See "Giving Back" at http://www.loreelough.com.) An active participant on most social media sites, Loree loves hearing from her readers, and answers every letter personally. Be sure to stop by and say hello on Facebook, Twitter, Pinterest, and Instagram!

CPSIA information can be obtained
at www.ICGtesting.com
Printed in the USA
LVOW03s0004170717
541361LV00001B/6/P